HEARTACHE IN HEELS

CATE LAWLEY

Copyright © 2019 Catherine G. Cobb
All rights reserved.

ALSO BY CATE LAWLEY

VEGAN VAMP MYSTERIES

Adventures of a Vegan Vamp

The Client's Conundrum

The Elvis Enigma

The Nefarious Necklace

The Halloween Haunting

The Selection Shenanigans

The Cupid Caper

The Reluctant Renfield

NIGHT SHIFT WITCH MYSTERIES

Night Shift Witch

Star of the Party

Tickle the Dragon's Tail

Twinkles Takes a Holiday

DEATH RETIRED

Death Retires

A Date with Death

On the Street Where Death Lives

FAIRMONT FINDS CANINE COZY MYSTERIES

On the Trail of a Killer

The Scent of a Poet's Past

Sniffing Out Sweet Secrets

Tracking a Poison Pen

CURSED CANDY MYSTERIES

Cutthroat Cupcakes

Twisted Treats

Fatal Fudge

Tea with a Demon: A Cursed Candy Short

Brunch with a Scurry of Squirrels: A Cursed Candy Short

LOVE EVER AFTER

Heartache in Heels

Skeptic in a Skirt

Pretty in Peep-Toes

Love Ever After Boxed Set One

LUCKY MAGIC

Lucky Magic

Luck of the Devil

Luck of the Draw

Wicked Bad Luck

For the most current listing of Cate's books, visit her website:

www.CateLawley.com

1
HILLARY

I wouldn't kill for the right wardrobe.

Maim? Possibly, but only for an old pair of jeans that would rock as cut-offs. Okay, that was a few seasons ago, but the point remains that while I love clothes (and shoes—let's not forget shoes), I'm not completely off my rocker.

My family, my friends, and an ex-boyfriend or two think I'm obsessed.

I say I'm committed.

As a professional shopper, it's literally my job. Granted, it's one of my many jobs...part-time personal shopper, part-time blogger, part-time dog walker, and part-time errand runner. I'm aware that's a lot of part-times, but a girl's gotta pay her bills, and —this is the important part—for at least part of the week, people *pay me to shop*.

Best. Job. Ever.

And also what brought me to my fave vintage and specialty clothing shop on this gorgeous morning.

I was at Every Woman's Fairy Godmother today because I needed to make my client feel fabulous.

The right slinky slip dress, one with silk lining and seams that felt like they weren't even there, could make a woman feel sexy.

But if my client needed the equivalent of a full-body hug, then stretchy skinny jeans (the kind that hide flaws instead of showcasing them) and an incredibly soft cotton tee paired with a hand-knit sweater might be the way to go.

That is the beauty of my job, the beauty of my *favorite* job. I can lift a client's mood with the right outfit, make her feel sexy or flirty or just a little more comfortable in her own skin. All I need is a good understanding of my client's needs, a decent sense of style, and a practically magical source of fab fashion.

Enter Madeleine and Every Woman's Fairy Godmother.

If I needed a special gown, a unique accessory, or a killer pair of heels, Madeleine waved her magical fashion wand and somehow made it happen. Her vintage store was always stocked with the classy, cutting-edge, nostalgic, hip, or beautifully tailored item I needed.

And on the rare occasions it wasn't in the store? She utilized her fairy godmother connections to hook me up with the piece I needed.

She had to have ridiculous connections to keep her shop stocked *and* fill all of the special orders that came her way. And the weirdest part? She had this crazy successful business that had been around for at least a decade, and I'd almost swear we were around the same age. Maybe she was over thirty and used great skincare products?

Forty seemed unlikely but not out of the realm of possibility, but then I'd catch her in a cute pair of jeans, a fitted tee, and almost no makeup—like today—and I'd bet the La Perla gift certificate I'd been hanging on to for a special occasion that she wasn't more than twenty-three.

She was that kind of woman, agelessly gorgeous, but occasionally mind-bogglingly youthful.

I could almost believe she was a magical fairy—except that was cra-cra.

"Hillary!" Madeleine called out with a cheery wave when she spotted me. "How's my second favorite client doing today?"

"Cute. You know I outclass Edgar in every way." I didn't. Not even close. Edgar was a full-time personal shopper with a posh client list I liked to drool over. He was also the wonderful man who'd turned me onto the best career ever and a great mentor.

Madeleine didn't argue, but she did give me a cheeky grin, letting me know that the day of me outclassing Edgar had most definitely not arrived.

Someday, I'd have enough of a client list to ditch the dog-walking and the errands. Maybe even the blogging, though I *really* enjoyed how flexible the blogging could be...

Someday, but not today. Today, I had a midday appointment with a chihuahua in possession of an itsy-bitsy bladder and a bark that could shatter glass.

Since I didn't want to clean up pee or upset Sugar, both of which would happen if I was even five minutes late, I retrieved my list from my bag and handed it to Madeleine. "I've got a few very special requests. Mrs. Peter Swinden."

We shared a look.

The list would most certainly be special-order items, hence my passing it along to Madeleine. Mrs. Peter Swinden didn't have taste that aligned with either Madeleine's or my own...or anyone else who would shop at Every Woman's Fairy Godmother. In fact, her requested items were invariably quite difficult to find, because Mrs. Peter Swinden's taste didn't align with most people's.

Oh, and the Mrs. Peter thing? I'm not making fun of my client. She actually introduces herself as Mrs. Peter Swinden. Who does that? Mrs. Peter Swinden, apparently.

While I couldn't be terribly finicky about my clients at this stage of my budding business's development, I would have cut Mrs. Peter and her truly terrible fashion sense loose, but for two facts: she paid ridiculously well, and she was an incredibly kind woman.

It was really the kindness. She was such a warm person. I enjoyed making her happy, even if it meant... My gaze flickered to the list Madeleine was now perusing, and I sighed. Yes, even if it meant finding a Mrs. Roper 1970s muumuu.

"The seventies have come back." I nodded, as if affirming the statement made the muumuu request less problematic. "A few times."

"Not this part of the seventies."

And that was kicker. Definitely not the Mrs. Roper muumuu part of the seventies. Except that part of the seventies had come back for Mrs. Peter Swinden. Or it would be shortly, because Madeleine would help me make it happen.

Mrs. Peter would get her muumuu, and she would be effervescent. Mrs. Peter happy was like a bottle of recently uncorked champagne. The cheap pink stuff, the kind that was fun and fizzy and shouldn't be saved for extra-special occasions but used to celebrate the everyday awesome of life.

And that was why Mrs. Peter was still my client.

Madeleine looked up from the list with an inscrutable expression. "Your time is coming."

I cocked my head, because I wasn't sure how to take that. I had faith in my business. All of my businesses, actually. I wasn't fearful success would pass me by, because I wouldn't let it. Managing my time, on the other hand, that was a different question, one that was starting to give me heartburn.

"You have other clients to shop for?" Madeleine asked, looking once again like her normal, helpful self.

I retrieved my cell from my purse then lifted it and said, "Yes. And since Sugar's bladder waits for no one, I'll get to it."

"All right, but pick something up for yourself today." As I started to decline, she pointed a finger at me. "Fifty percent off whatever you find. Do it."

Even though I was a bit tight for cash this month, I felt compelled to "do it." Looked like I was doing a little shopping for myself.

Did it get colder in here? The air conditioning must have kicked on, because my entire body shivered.

2

HILLARY

I started with the shoes.

Naturally, because shoes.

Sadly, no heels, platforms, wedges, or sandals called my name today, and I wouldn't use that fifty percent just to use it. I had to find a special piece, something that begged to go home with me. Something that would brighten my day. Actually, something that would brighten many days.

Since I wasn't finding a special pair of gorgeous heels to brighten this and many more days to come, I retrieved my client list from my phone and started the hunt.

I had five client requests to address over the next few days, and three of them could potentially be filled at Every Woman's Fairy Godmother: an evening bag to coordinate with a pair of shoes I'd already sourced through a boutique across town; a necklace to accent one client's "ladies" (she was keen for her husband to take more interest in that particular part of her anatomy and, resultingly, she hoped, their sex life); and a flashy but not-too-flashy eighties party dress for a client who wanted to shine at her eighties-themed reunion (she hadn't graduated in the eighties, rather two decades later, and her idea of eighties-themed ran toward tulle and Madonna).

Some days my job felt a teensy bit therapy adjacent, since I was listening to my clients' problems and then offering up articles of clothing to address them.

The dress seemed the practical first choice. My client was a size four, not always the easiest size to find in vintage stores, unless I was hunting for something from a few decades earlier. If the racks didn't yield something suitable, I'd add it to the request list I'd provided Madeleine.

But victory was mine!

I found just the piece, and in such pristine condition that it couldn't possibly have survived a drunken prom night. After checking the seams and zipper, looking for any tears in the tulle (so, so much tulle), and whipping out my tape measure to verify the size ran true, I had a winner.

Before heading to the counter to drop off my find, I made a quick pit stop at the bags, where I scored my second gorgeous find, a gold brocade bag that would complement the shoes I'd already purchased.

"You look like you've done well." Madeleine eyed the bag fondly as she took it from me and wrapped it in tissue paper. "I always liked this one. It's elegance with a splash of fun. And speaking of fun..." She gathered the dress and its short, multilayered skirt in her arms, then ran her finger across the lettering on the belt. It read "Boy Toy," which matched my client's sense of humor to a tee.

I was about to reply—something about how I always found exactly the right thing in Madeleine's shop—when a pair of glasses in the display case caught my eye.

The gaudiest vintage cat-eyed sunglasses I'd ever seen sparkled up at me. Encrusted with crystals, they looked like they'd been bedazzled by an overzealous twelve-year-old, and I adored them.

"Gimme" was going through my head, but I managed to articulate a slightly more polite request to see them.

Madeleine blinked at the bling, then retrieved them. "The frames are original, from the fifties. It's just the tinted glass that are new. Removing the prescription makes them functional again."

"Practical."

Madeleine grinned at my comment.

Okay, no, there was nothing practical about the glitzy glasses, but they were adorable and needed to be mine.

She quoted me a price that included the discount, and when I nodded my agreement, she packed the glasses and the ridiculously sparkly and completely impractical case that accompanied them together with my other purchases.

It wasn't until I was already in my car and headed to prevent a Sugar pee disaster that I realized I'd forgotten to look at the necklaces.

My client's bosom would have to wait another day or two to be admired. Not a tragedy, and I still had a few days before the promised delivery date—but I wasn't usually quite so forgetful when it came to my businesses.

3

HILLARY

Sugar got her walk, and her house was pee-free. Victory!

It was a tricky proposition, because if I came any earlier and her owner happened to be running a little late in the evening—yep, pee disaster.

Poor Sugar. She really needed two walks during the day, which I wasn't capable of providing. I needed to have a talk with her owner (again) and tell her she needed to hire a different service (again).

On one hand, achievement unlocked and yay for me. I'd grown my dog-walking business to the point that I was turning away new clients. I'd stopped advertising over a year ago, but I still got referrals.

But on the other hand, my other businesses were

growing as well, and I had to start making some choices.

Choices were hard.

I'd straddled the line of too busy for a while now. Fear of missing a mortgage payment will do that to a gal. But if I was being honest with myself, it wasn't really a financial fear that pushed me. It was a different worry altogether. By choosing to focus on one or two of my businesses, I was leaving the others behind—and I liked my little moneymaking projects.

Dog walking kept me fit, and I loved my time with the pooches. I didn't have one of my own (with my schedule? Um, no), so client walks fulfilled all my doggie needs. Without my dog-walking biz, I might have to actually commit to a pet to get my canine fix.

My gofering gig tied in neatly with my personal shopping biz, and, in fact, had overlapping clientele. So it just made sense to keep the errand running rolling.

Which left my fashion blogging, a business that was just starting to gain some revenue potential, nicely complemented my personal shopping business, and had the greatest flexibility scheduling-wise.

Ugh. I needed more hours in the day, not fewer jobs.

I wanted to keep them all.

The other thing I wanted to keep? Some semblance of a social life, even if that social life was limited to a few friends and my grandfather.

My grandfather was the one easy choice in my life. I'd always make time for my favorite person. Gramps was the best.

Speaking of my favorite guy, I was headed to check on him today. I glanced at my GPS and saw I was just a few minutes away.

When my grandmother died three years ago, he'd had a hard time. In the interim, he'd made exceptional progress...mostly.

He'd bounced from complete, grief-stricken, twenty-four-hour-housecoat-wearing depression, to...Brad.

Brad.

I tapped my fingers on the steering wheel of my Fiat.

Brad was a problem.

One that might cost my grandfather his freedom if I didn't keep a close watch.

The sun busted out from behind the clouds, and I pulled out my nifty new glasses. Just looking at their sparkly frames made me smile and—temporarily—forget about Brad.

Steering with one hand, I ran my fingers over the bumpy stones with the other.

The fifties had such a flair for fashion and an appreciation of glamour. They might not have had gel manicures or comfortably functional undergarments, and there had been some seriously bad dye jobs happening back in the day, but, overall, the fifties were a fashion plus in my book.

I slipped the glasses on and was pleasantly surprised by their quality. Whoever had replaced the lenses had done a bang-up job. The view through my windshield was crisp and clear.

"Thank you, Madeleine."

With a glance at my dashboard clock, I confirmed I had plenty of time for dinner with Gramps before my first evening appointment.

Gramps and I needed to talk. About Brad—I couldn't help rolling my eyes heavenward, Lord give me strength—but also about my sneaky, conniving aunt and uncle. Every time I thought of them, the back of my neck itched. They'd been quiet lately—too quiet. Mischief was afoot.

The plotting duo would have a field day if I took my eye off the prize for any length of time. The prize being Gramps' freedom and happiness. Unfortunately, my grandfather had way too much faith in his kids' good intentions.

I turned into Gramps' neighborhood. I checked on him two or three times a week. Not that he wasn't completely capable of caring for himself. Just the opposite. He walked a mile twice a day, had better eyesight than most seventy-five-year-olds, and cooked a much meaner meal than me. But there was Brad and my evil, overbearing family to worry about.

After I pulled into Gramps' driveway and parked, I leaned my head back against the headrest and closed my eyes.

If the house wasn't worth so much (that dang east Austin gentrification), if my aunt and uncle would spend a little more time with Gramps, if everyone in my family would accept that Gramps' house meant the world to him, if everyone would stop for a moment to consider what the loss of my grandfather's independence would do to him...

Who was I kidding? Even if all those things were true, that didn't get rid of Brad.

I slipped my fingers under my new shades and pressed the inside corners of my eyes, trying to stem the sudden desire to cry like a broken-hearted tween. I was not a crier, and Gramps would spot my red eyes in a heartbeat.

For an old man with an imaginary friend, my grandfather really had it together. His memory was sharp, he was physically fit, and his cognition seemed unimpaired by age...minus Brad.

The business with Brad started about three years ago. Every once in a while, Gramps would mention his buddy Brad. At first, we all thought he'd made a friend in the neighborhood. (Except for my mom, who thought Gramps had a boyfriend.) Given my grandmother's passing and Gramps' ensuing depression, I'd been thrilled. Neighbor friend, boyfriend—whoever Brad was to Gramps, I was happy because he was happy.

And I kept on being thrilled right up until I realized Brad wasn't a neighbor friend or a boyfriend. Brad was an *imaginary* friend. A figment of a lonely widower's overactive imagination.

I wigged out—at first. I thought for sure that the dreaded D or A (dementia, Alzheimer's—even thinking the words made my eyes burn) were around the corner, that Brad was a hallucination or a sign of diminishing cognition, and it broke my heart.

But then I'd done my due diligence, and I don't mean internet research. I talked with his doctor, expressed my concern, and asked what I, as his closest relative, should do to monitor the situation.

It had taken a good six months, but I'd eventually become convinced that Brad was Gramps' only hallucination—and a weirdly helpful one, at that.

After Brad showed up, Gramps picked up his daily walks again. He'd stopped when my grandmother had become ill. He also started to grocery-shop weekly, when he'd been a bulk, once-a-month shopper before. And this was really strange: his diet changed. He started eating more fresh foods and less canned and prepackaged stuff. My Gramps came from the generation of canned food. If his imaginary friend could do what I couldn't—convince him to adopt a healthier lifestyle—then I was Team Brad.

So what if Gramps, in his loneliness, had made up a really cool friend to keep him company? It was three years into the two's surreal friendship, and Brad only seemed to have been a good influence... minus the part where he wasn't real.

My family, especially Aunt Carol and Uncle Tim, didn't share my viewpoint, so I discouraged him from speaking about Brad with the rest of the greedy, retirement-home-loving family. They wanted Gramps' house sold, and Gramps in a tiny apartment with a bunch of older people who weren't nearly as fit as he was.

That might be the right answer, possibly even a really fun place for him to live—at some point. Not yet, and only if it was his choice.

Because Gramps *loved* his home.

Mom and Dad weren't a problem. They lived out of state, so just about everything to do with Gramps flew over their heads. (Mom still thought Brad was Gramps' boyfriend, just his imaginary boyfriend.)

But Aunt Carol and Uncle Tim lived locally, and they were a problem. Call me a cynic, but I suspected the steadily increasing value of Gramps' old house had something to do with Carol and Tim's recent escalating interest in placing him in a home.

Of course, they didn't call it a home, and they swore he'd love living there.

Right. Just like he'd love it when the new owners demolished the home he'd lived in all of his adult life.

Unfortunately, it was the property that was valuable, because renovating a dated three-thousand-square-foot house from the fifties would cost much more than tearing it down and throwing up a box mansion twice that size.

A tap on my car window about made me pee my pants. No bueno, since this vintage skirt was one of my faves.

When my heart stopped galloping, I rolled the window down.

"Sorry, Gramps. Lost in admiration of my new nail color. What do you think?" I flashed him what was actually a three-day-old manicure.

He squinted, a sure sign of an attempt to think of something positive, then said, "Very shiny. How about a little dinner? That *is* why you're here, isn't it? So I can feed you?" He started back inside the house without waiting for a response.

And that was another Brad bonus. Brad had not only converted Gramps to fresher foods, he'd taught

Gramps how to cook. And by "how to cook," I mean how to cook really good food.

Weird, right? But when Brad worked for the forces of good, it was hard to hold his nonexistence against him.

I rolled up my window, checked my mascara and eyeliner surreptitiously for smearing in the rearview mirror, and then hopped out of the car. Jogging up behind him, I said, "You know I'm all about a free meal."

Once inside, Gramps gave me a big hug. "Always good to see you, peanut."

He waited until we'd finished our meal and were having an after-dinner espresso made with his fancy, ultra-modern espresso machine—thanks, Brad—to spring his bad news. "I've got an appointment with some lady doctor next week."

I tapped a nail on the table. "A lady doctor, huh? Not just a doctor?"

Since common sense ruled out a gynecologist, I could only assume he literally meant a doctor who was a woman. As modern as he could be, in some ways he was a stodgy old dude. Also, I knew for a fact that his GP was a man, so... "Why the new doctor?"

"Tim and Carol thought—"

"Whoa. Tim and Carol? Is your new lady doctor a psychiatrist?" Because if she was, I could not be held accountable for any action taken against my nutty relatives. Their evil ways were driving me mad.

"Calm down. Hey, put your phone away. It was either go voluntarily or have the court require an evaluation. We don't want that, do we? It's better this way."

I stopped cruising my contacts for Aunt Carol's number. "*Is* it better? Do you know that for sure? I think we should hire an attorney."

Grandpa leaned back in his 1976 kitchen chair and crossed his arms. "No."

Zen.

That was me.

Deep breathing, happy thoughts... I would not murder my aunt and uncle. I would not murder my aunt and uncle. I would not— "Ugh. I'm gonna kill them."

"No. Whatever you're thinking or scheming"—he gave me an intent look—"and I know it's not actual murder, just stop. I'm doing the evaluation. It's no problem, because I'm not crazy."

I knew where this conversation was going. Tim and Carol were family. He loved them, they loved him, they certainly didn't mean any harm. Blah, blah, blah.

My rear, they didn't mean him any harm.

What else was tossing him in an old folks' home but harm? An active, healthy, with-it guy like

Gramps should only move to a retirement community if he wanted to. And the dynamic duo had hardly gone with an active seniors' retirement community. No, what they'd picked out was an old folks' home for the mentally not-quite-all-there.

Also, small problem: Gramps *was* a teensy-weensy bit crazy. Not couldn't-look-after-himself crazy, but he wasn't exactly pass-a-psych-exam sane either. The dude had an imaginary friend, and he wasn't five.

But I couldn't say that.

"It's not about whether you're crazy or not. It's about whether you can make responsible financial decisions for yourself, Gramps, and whether you can care for yourself." Which was what it *should* be about, but I was really worried it wouldn't be. Also, much as I hated to say it out loud... "I'm afraid they'll trick you."

He uncrossed his arms, and his eyes softened. "Am I so gullible?"

I groaned. "Not gullible. But you're a stand-up guy, and you can't lie to save your life."

A wounded look crossed his face.

"Gramps. Real talk, now. You couldn't tell me my nail polish looks nice, even though I know you wanted to. If Brad comes up—and you know he will—you won't be able to fudge. And any talk of Brad and y'all's exploits will put your credibility in doubt."

Gramps brightened at the mention of Brad. "Did I show you my new phone? Brad helped me pick it out." He pulled his phone out. He'd already upgraded to a smartphone from his previous flip version a few years ago—with Brad's help, because *I* hadn't been able to convince him—so I wasn't completely shocked to find him sporting a cutting-edge phone.

My best guess was that Gramps had begun to plumb the depths of the internet, which meant he'd quite possibly discovered review sites and video-streaming sites and forums. How else had he found and learned to use all of his new gadgets? Prior to my grandmother's death, he'd never been high-tech, and now he was frothing milk with his fancy steamer and sporting a phone even I envied.

The other option, that his imaginary friend was real, wasn't exactly an option.

"Don't look that way."

Since I'd been staring off into space, I hadn't a clue how I looked.

Gramps frowned. "You have that look, the one you get when you're thinking too hard or hormonal."

My jaw dropped. Not literally, but seriously—since when did Gramps start calling me out on my PMS symptoms? And yes, I did get just a touch emotional during that particular time of the month, but who could blame me? Some of the commercials they play on TV these days are real tearjerkers.

I pointed a finger at him. "I love you, but no more talking about my hormones." I cut him off as he was about to reply. "And don't blame Brad."

Gramps shrugged.

He'd totally been about to blame Brad.

Which just proved my point: Brad was a problem. For a friend who wasn't real, his influence was incredibly pervasive. He'd inserted himself into practically every aspect of Gramps' life.

Which made my stomach churn, because there wasn't a chance in hell Gramps could pass a psych eval.

"Oh, Gramps. You see the issue, right? Your imaginary friend is steering your buying decisions. You know and I know that you're not going to spend all your money on some pyramid scheme or some other scam, but do you understand how listening to the advice of a guy who doesn't exist might be a red flag for a psychiatrist who's evaluating your ability to make responsible financial choices?"

"It'll be fine, peanut. You worry too much."

He pulled me into a hug, and as comforting as it felt to be wrapped up in a bear hug by one of the people I loved most in the world, I also knew that it meant the conversation was over.

Gramps wasn't going to lie about Brad.

He wasn't going to hire an attorney who would protect his interests.

He *was* going to show up for that appointment with the psychiatrist.

And it would *not* go well.

4

BRAD

I no longer crept from room to room, worrying the unexpected sight of me would give Walter a heart attack. I hadn't in years.

Walter knew my incorporeal self didn't make much noise, so my seemingly sudden appearances weren't actually all that sudden, and he'd grown accustomed to my catlike ways.

In fact, we'd had a few philosophical conversations pondering the meaning of me.

How could I speak and be heard when I had no physical presence?

How could Walter hear and see me, but no one else could?

Why didn't I have any memory prior to the short time I'd wandered the city before meeting Walter?

Who had I been before I'd become Brad, Walter's BFF?

And here was the humdinger: what was I?

We'd landed on ghost as the best guess, but I didn't feel ghostly. I felt…lost, confused, frustrated.

I didn't feel dead.

That particular part I'd kept to myself, because I recognized how crazy it sounded. I walked through walls, had a conscious mind with no substantial body, and could only be seen by a seventy-five-year-old widower who'd been in the midst of a depressive spiral when I showed up on his lawn.

If I faced reality—a reality infused with a stout belief in the otherworldly—I was a ghost.

A ghost whose existence would be significantly worse without the companionship of a pretty amazing guy. And right now, that guy was looking pretty stressed out.

"Walter."

The lines of worry on his forehead faded away when he looked up from his empty whiskey glass. As soon as his granddaughter had left, he'd poured himself a finger of his favorite and planted himself at the kitchen table.

He needed a few minutes to process, but he'd had that. Time to start facing facts.

"She's concerned." I watched him refill his glass and then toast me, which sparked a memory. Cool liquid on my tongue, the warm bite of liquor as it slid down my throat.

Those little memories would crop up occasionally. Small hints of my corporeal preferences. It seemed I'd liked my whiskey on the rocks. Walter would not approve.

He picked up the glass and headed to the sink, where he proceeded to load the dishwasher. "She shouldn't be so worried. I'm fitter now than I was three years ago." He didn't look up as he continued with his task.

Three years ago. Not a time pulled at random from the rich, full life of Walter Barrett. A little over three years ago, Walter's wife Ingrid had passed after a very short and painful illness. An aggressive form of brain cancer, he'd told me once.

He never spoke of her illness, except for that one time. When he did talk about Ingrid, it was always his favorite memories of her. She sounded like an incredible woman, and I could hear his love for her shining through in the stories he told.

That was today.

Three years ago, Walter hadn't been in a very good place and certainly hadn't been discussing his recently deceased wife.

When I'd stumbled onto his lawn, I'd gotten an almost comically stereotypical response: "Get off my lawn. There's a sidewalk for a reason."

Instead of removing my incorporeal self from his lawn, I'd jumped up and down and screamed like a lunatic. I'd been halfway to *becoming* a lunatic at the time, so it was no great surprise I'd acted like one.

"Are you high?" a grumpy, unkempt, robe-wearing Walter had asked.

At which point I'd stopped jumping and asked him if *he* was. Of the two of us, that was the much more likely scenario. I might have been invisible to almost every human on earth, but I wasn't the one loitering on the lawn in a bathrobe and slippers while sporting an ungroomed overgrowth of whiskers.

Walter had looked rough, bordering on homeless.

The very not-scruffy Walter of the present waved his hand in front of my face. "Anyone home in there?"

"Huh?"

"You think I'm not doing better these days?" Walter's lips tipped up slightly in amusement as he rinsed another dish. "I have proof that I am. I keep a journal with all of my personal habits, because someone threatened to scare the pants off me regularly if I didn't."

"You're welcome." Because that journal, while no longer necessary, had been the key piece of evidence I'd used to initiate significant change in Walter's life.

A guy who didn't shower regularly, rarely shaved, and never left the house probably wasn't doing great, and he hadn't been able to argue against the evidence written in his own hand.

He'd also been ready for some help. He'd wanted to pull himself out of the funk he was in, but he hadn't known how to do it and had been too proud to ask his family for help.

"Yeah. You know I appreciate it. I did then, and I still do now."

"Then listen to me, and listen to Hillary. This appointment with the shrink is going to be a problem. You can't have an imaginary friend, Walter. People start talking dementia, Alzheimer's, schizophrenia, crazy old guy. Any label that lets them explain why you're seeing and hearing things that no one else can. I don't think it'll matter that you're otherwise completely rational."

"Call it what it is, son: hallucinating." Walter looked over his shoulder, meeting my gaze. "And no one would think I'm losing my mind if you'd show yourself to the rest of the world."

"We've talked about this. I promise, Walter, I've tried. And tried and tried. I don't know why, but you're it; you're the only one who can see me. I love you, man, but having only one person to talk to for three years? Come on. That's not how I'd choose to live."

"Being dead stinks," Walter said.

"Amen to that." I couldn't argue, even if I didn't feel the least bit dead.

Walter hypothesized it was my inability to let go—of life, of a particular person, of a certain problem—that continued to tether me to this plane of existence. Maybe he was right, because I sure as hell wasn't ready to have my existence wiped from the face of the planet, even if that existence was less than satisfactory.

Walter and I shared that desire. We both wanted to live.

Now.

Three years ago, it had taken some wheedling on my part to remind him how important his life—even one without Ingrid—was, and that there was still joy to be found in a world without her.

We'd walked together, shared stories, watched TV, hung out. And after a few months of exceptional Brad one-on-one time (hey, I'm a great guy, even if I don't have a physical body or any sort of memory), Walter had gotten fitter, healthier, and happier. His depressive funk faded to something he'd live through rather than being something he was living day to day.

Win-win. Walter was a great guy, and we both had needed a buddy to get us through a rough patch.

My rough patch—death—just happened to be a little more permanent.

Walter retrieved his glass from the counter and poured himself another finger. "Still wonder why that psychic gal couldn't see you."

"Maybe she was a fake." And even though it made my nonexistent neck itch, I said, "Maybe we should try again. A different one, though."

The last one had been full of it. I couldn't believe that Hillary, who was usually so sensible when it came to her Gramps, had invited that charlatan into Walter's home.

Side note: I might be ever so slightly biased where Hillary was concerned. Hillary was smoking. As in seriously hot. And while I didn't have a body, I still *felt* like I had a body. So I tended to see Hillary in a positive light, basically all of the time.

But she was legit great. Even if she weren't super hot, I'd still be into her. She was just this amazing girl. Ambitious but always making time for family. Sweet, but practical. And so kind.

Walter cleared his throat and eyed me over his whiskey glass. "You had that look."

"What look?" I knew what look. The I've-got-the-hots-for-your-granddaughter look. Oops. Before he could describe my infatuated expression—something I didn't want to have to explain—I turned the conversation back to paranormal problem solving. "Maybe Hillary's new psychic would come to the house. What's her name? Mary Jane?" I took a seat across from Walter at the kitchen table.

However this ghost stuff worked, I was glad I had just enough ectoplasm (or whatever made up what little physical presence I had) to interact with physical objects. The idea of hovering for eternity made me queasy. It would be even better if I could lift something beyond a feather. A small feather. My life kinda sucked minus Walter.

Walter scratched his day-old beard. After he'd reestablished all his daily grooming habits, I'd convinced him that he didn't have to shave *every* day, that the ladies liked a little scruff. Whether that was true for Walter's age bracket, I didn't know, but I was sick of watching the guy nick himself. How could a man shave for more than fifty years and be so bad at it?

"It's Mary Margaret. She sounds like a nun, not a bad habit." Walter pinched his thumb and forefinger together and made as if he was smoking weed. It was pretty hilarious. "But I don't know. Hillary said this one doesn't see ghosts, just auras."

"Okay. Maybe I have an aura. I could have one of those, right?" Since I could barely pronounce it and definitely didn't know what an aura was, I figured it could go either way. Anyway... "This psychic seems less shady. Even the name is solid. I mean, Mary Margaret? You're sure she's not a nun?"

"Ha! A psychic nun. No, I don't think so." Walter shook his head and chuckled. "I have to say, before meeting you, I always thought Hillary was a little loony with her psychics and her crystals and tarot. Guess I was wrong about some of that stuff." He took a sip of whiskey, then said, "Yeah, okay. I'll ask her. This Mary Margaret does seem like a straight shooter from everything Hillary says about her. Now, that Madame Celeste, she was another story altogether."

We shared a glance. I'd say she was nutty, but Madame Celeste had left me with the feeling that she didn't buy everything she was selling. In fact, she'd seemed more in touch with her bank account than her spiritual side.

Walter continued to sip his whiskey. He'd make it last, because two was his limit, but watching him enjoy the drink was painful. It made me feel like a toddler, the kind that held out his hands and said, "Gimme, gimme, gimme." This toddler wasn't getting whiskey anytime soon, and if my instincts were wrong and I was truly dead, then never again.

After we'd wallowed in silence—Walter knew I craved earthly things like booze and good food (though he hadn't a clue I was half in love with his granddaughter) and left me to my misery when I chose to hang out while he imbibed—he said, "It's hard not to talk about you. We spend a lot of time together."

I shrugged.

Walter raised his bushy—but now neatly trimmed—eyebrows. "A lot."

"Yeah, that's true." I thanked God (or whoever was pulling the threads on the tapestry of my fate) every day for Walter.

Before I'd stumbled on Walter in his previously unkempt and depressed state, I'd been homeless, nameless, and completely without hope. Walter had given me a name and a home, but more than that—Walter had given me purpose. Life had been grim in those months before meeting my roommate.

I appreciated the guy and didn't want him squirreled away in a depressing old folks' home. Granted, the place his kid had picked out didn't look terrible, but it was still a home. It was intended for seniors with deteriorating mental faculties, and that wasn't Walter.

Also, the guy loved—seriously *loved*—his house. It would break his heart to be forced out, and his kids should know that. Hillary understood.

But I'd shared my opinion about the shrink, and since Walter's mind was sharp as a tack, there was no need to badger the man. He'd make up his own mind in the end—as he should.

"Hey," I said, "didn't you want me to show you that audiobook app for your new phone?"

Walter smacked his hand on the table. "That's right. I left it on my dresser. Give me a minute to fetch it." Walter took another sip of his whiskey, and then left to fetch his phone. He was always leaving it somewhere in the house.

As he disappeared, I made a note to bring up Mary Margaret again. Even though I worried a true medium might send me on my way—out of Walter's life, onto the next stage of my own, into the great beyond?—there was still the possibility that a person with true talent might be able to see me.

And while it might not be the best option for my future, it might help save Walter's.

5

HILLARY

"Gramps. She's not a psychic nun, just a psychic. Where do you get this stuff? Wait, don't tell me. Brad." I shifted the phone to my other ear and continued to scrub the dish in my sink.

"You said it, not me. So? Will you call your lady friend, the one who isn't a nun, and have her come over?"

Gramps seemed convinced this time would be different. I hated to disappoint him, but it would be exactly the same as before, because *there was no Brad.* "I'll talk to her, but I don't think—"

"You're an angel, peanut. Dinner the day after tomorrow?"

"Wouldn't miss it." I viciously scrubbed a particularly resistant bit of food, then blinked when I noticed my gloveless hands in the soapy water. My cuticles would hate me later for my absent-mindedness. Also, I probably wouldn't have to scrub if I didn't leave my dishes in the sink for a day or two at a time.

"Great. I'll tell you all about this new app I got. I can walk and listen to a book at the same time on my new phone. I'm still trying to decide on the earbuds or the over-ear headphones. I think over-ear. They have better sound quality."

My lips twitched. Even if his imaginary friend Brad was the bane of my existence, he'd been an amazing influence on Gramps. I *loved* seeing my grandfather doing so well, because, well, I loved my grandfather.

There was a time when I didn't think anything could pull him back into the land of the living. And his acceptance of relatively modern tech was mind-boggling. Audiobooks, so he could listen to books on his walks. My heart swelled with warm, fuzzy feelings.

"I love you, Gramps."

"I love you too, peanut. Does that mean you don't have an opinion about which headphones?"

"Nope. You go with your gut." Or Brad's recommendation...but I wasn't going there. "I'll see you day after tomorrow for dinner."

He grunted his affirmation, then said, "Call your psychic. Don't forget."

"Yes, sir." After I ended the call, my hand hovered over the contacts icon, but then I changed my mind and put the phone down. I said I'd call, but not *when*.

I finished the dishes and even remembered to put my gloves on so my manicurist wouldn't give me the evil eye. After a little blogging, finishing up with my client emails for the day, and reviewing my calendar for the rest of the week, it was already time for bed. The hours of every day snuck by faster and faster, especially on evenings I had after-hour clients, and I'd had two tonight.

Scheduling would continue to be an issue, so long as I continued to juggle four growing businesses.

But it was a problem I didn't want to think about right now.

Just as I was about to get into bed, my phone chirped with a text from my BFF Beth. Speaking of not having time, I couldn't remember the last time we'd had a girls' night.

I flicked the message open. *Have I told you about the weird dreams I've been having?*

This was not a text-response kind of message. I hit the dial icon and didn't even wait for a hello before I said, "I want all the details."

"You perv." She was laughing when she said it, but she wasn't wrong.

I was completely perving out. That was what happened when a healthy woman in her twenties went without sex for... "Holy bananas. It's been almost a year since what's-his-name."

Beth snorted. "What's-his-name? You mean your last boyfriend? And you wonder why it didn't last."

Except she was wrong about that: I didn't wonder. Not even a little bit. I'd known right away he wasn't The One, but I'd also known that he'd be a fun for-now guy. And since he'd felt the same, we parted on excellent terms.

"Sean, that was his name." No need to dwell on the fact that we hadn't kept in touch, or that it had taken a solid mental effort on my part to remember his name.

"Should I pat you on the back that you remember the name of the man you dated for four months?" The crinkle of plastic packaging traveled with devious precision across the cell line.

"Please tell me you're not eating rice cakes."

"Ok, I won't. Anyhoo, my dream—which was not pervy, thank you very much—was completely weird."

"Much as I want to hear about your dream"—although less so now than before, since I knew it wasn't a sex dream—"I'd much rather hear about the Pringles you're eating." Dang it, those didn't come in a plastic bag. "Sorry, the Cheetos. Or maybe the Funyuns?"

Hope sprang eternal when it came to my vicarious enjoyment of carbs.

I was minimizing my carb intake these days, and while that single decision had upped my energy, thereby allowing me to put off any decisions about my businesses for a little while longer, I had wicked-sharp cravings for salty snacks.

"Funyuns, Hillary? Do you seriously eat those? Does anyone eat those?"

Beth was my best friend in the world, but sometimes her food choices made me second-guess her place in my life. Rice cakes—just yuck.

"You don't? What's wrong with you?"

"I'm not answering that. Also, have a few Cheetos before you lose your mind. A few more days on a healthy diet and your system will be so shocked that you'll start seeing Brad."

I groaned.

Brad. It was like my life was revolving around him.

What was I going to do about Brad? Or, more accurately, what was I going to do about my grandfather's hallucination? I really shouldn't think about him as if he was a real guy.

"I can't find anything online about a Brad-type

imaginary friend. Everything I've seen is really sad and deals with seniors who have a host of other problems. Gramps just had a physical about four months ago, and he's fit, thinks clearly, and seems completely fine. And trust me, I was very involved in the process and talked to his doctor. He's doing great."

"He's doing great, minus the guy who gives him advice and keeps him company. The one who isn't really there."

"Yep, minus that." I groaned again. "Brad stopped walking with him, because he didn't want people to see Gramps talking to himself, so—get this, Brad hooked him up with an audiobook app on his phone. Gramps is all excited about walking again."

Beth made a small, distressed sound. "Man, that stinks. Brad sounds like a really nice guy."

"Right? But you don't know the worst of it. Aunt Carol and Uncle Tim have scheduled a psych eval."

"What?" Beth hollered. "Honey, I'm so sorry. They really want him out of that house, don't they?"

"It's so weird. Neither of them is hurting for cash, and they swear they have his best interests at heart, but..."

"You're not so sure you believe them."

I loosened the death grip I'd taken of my cell, switched hands, and stretched my cramped fingers. "If they bothered to spend more time with him, I might. Or if they trusted my opinion, as the person who spends the *most* time with him, I might."

"Uh..." Beth cleared her throat delicately. "The most outside of Brad."

"Not helping."

"No, what's not helping is how many hours you work. Get rid of your dog-walking business." She interrupted me when I started to protest. "Or your blogging gig. Something's gonna give."

"I'm working on it."

"Yeah, Hills, and I'll believe you when you say that like you mean it. But for now, get a good night's sleep. Everything will look better in the morning."

She was right. Not a solution to my many woes, but being well rested would help keep me healthy and sane.

When I ended the call, I realized I never had heard about Beth's odd dream.

Not the end of the world, since it had probably been an excuse to check in with me. Her healthy eating habits aside, Beth was good people.

6

HILLARY

I woke to a nasty feeling of something forgotten. It was a dark cloud that weighed on me and made me even grumpier than normal. For clarification, that's seriously grumpy. I am not a morning person.

Had I missed someone's birthday? Failed to take out the trash bins? No-showed for a client appointment?

Something had slipped through the gaps, and my subconscious wasn't gonna let it slide.

By the time my alarm went off three minutes later, I had an inkling as to what might be causing the guilt-fest that was ruining my under-the-covers, bed-wallowing snuggle time.

I needed to call my psychic. I'd promised

Gramps, but I'd dodged the commitment yesterday in hopes of postponing everyone's disappointment.

Time to get this day started. If I was calling Mary Margaret first thing—and I was, or the guilt would only snowball and give me an even bigger case of the grumps—then I needed to get a dose of caffeine in me.

Seven minutes later, coffee in hand, I made the call.

Mary Margaret answered with a cheerful greeting. Mary Margaret was a morning person. I tried not to hold that against her.

"It's Hillary, and I've got a huge favor to ask."

"Since it's before nine and we both know you're not at your best in the morning, I already knew that before I picked up the phone." I could hear the smile in Mary Margaret's voice.

Mary Margaret was solid. Grounded, practical, and unflappable. She exuded calm, and even seemed to transfer her sense of well-being to those around her.

Gramps would love her.

"I've told you about my grandfather."

"You have," she agreed in an amiable tone.

I sucked down more java in hopes it would make my end of this conversation more coherent. "And I think I've mentioned Brad?"

"Your grandfather's invisible roommate? Oh, yes."

"I don't think I told you that I had a psychic come out to the house."

"To meet Brad?" And she managed to say it without sounding judgmental. Mary Margaret was a gem.

"Well, mostly to *not* meet Brad and to convince Gramps that Brad wasn't real."

"But a tiny part of you hoped your psychic would find some evidence."

I blew out a breath. "Yep. Lady, you know me too well."

"I know that Brad—or the construct that your grandfather has created and calls Brad—has had a positive impact on the quality of your grandfather's life, so it's not odd that you'd hope Brad was real."

"Yes, but she didn't find anything."

"And you used someone who advertised themselves as a medium?" Mary Margaret cleared her throat. "Someone reliable?"

"Hard to say. I found her online." My lips twitched at the indelicate snort my comment elicited. "Either way, this psychic medium didn't convince Gramps of anything, and now he wants you."

"Oh." With one word, she conveyed her dismay. "You know I don't do ghosts."

"I know. I was hoping you'd put aside your ethics for the greater good. Just one visit, have a look around, see if anything pings your radar."

She laughed. "Pings my radar, huh?"

"Don't tell me you don't have radar. You may not be a ghost expert, but you're already ten times better than Madame Celeste." I smiled, and I knew she'd hear it in my voice. "You're trustworthy, Mary Margaret."

Which elicited a groan. Because she was. One hundred percent. Mary Margaret was well aware of her chosen field's reputation. She maintained high ethical standards, because that was how she rolled—but also because she wanted to improve the public's perception.

Since she hadn't declined—yet—I said, "I've already told Gramps that you do auras, that your expertise lies with the living, not the dead."

"If I do agree, it would be with your grandfather's understanding that I claim no particular talent as a medium?"

"Yes." Since my coffee was cooling, I had a few more gulps. "I'll make sure he completely understands that, but I did already tell him."

"You know, assuming Brad does exist, he wouldn't have an aura, because he's not alive. Dead people don't have auras, and that's why I'm no medium."

I was so close to convincing her. Sure, she didn't have the absolute best skill set for the supernatural part of this gig, but she met the most important requirement: I trusted her completely. Also, the woman had intuition like no other.

And I'd tell Gramps both of those things. Hopefully, he'd listen to sense when Mary Margaret told him she got no pings on her supernatural radar, and that would inch him that much closer to the reality of Brad's nonexistence.

"So, are you going to do a stressed-out granddaughter a solid?" When she didn't agree right away, I decided it was time to fess up to the reality of the situation. "My aunt and uncle have set up a psych exam for him next week. I'm fairly confident it's the first step in having him declared incompetent."

"Oh, Hillary. I'm so sorry." She paused and then, in a very quiet voice, said, "And you're sure that's not the best outcome in this situation?"

"I'm absolutely certain. I know the whole Brad thing makes my Gramps sound like a loon, but he's otherwise completely with it. I see him a few times a week. I *know* him—unlike the craptastic dynamic duo."

"Hillary," Mary Margaret said. "They're his children. They're concerned, or they wouldn't be doing this."

I got where she was coming from, but if they

were really so darned worried about their father, why didn't they get off their duffs and meet the man for dinner every week or two? Were their lives so very busy they couldn't do that? And it wasn't like it was a hardship. Gramps was awesome. He was great company.

"K, I'm gonna admit to some biases in this particular area, but I'm not so sure that Uncle Tim and Aunt Carol's motives are as golden as you think they are."

Mary Margaret sighed. "I'll do it."

I quietly did a fist pump, then thanked her profusely. I might have to celebrate with one of the last few donuts stashed in my freezer. I'd earned one, because this was a hard conversation for a non-morning person to have before noon. "When do you think you might swing by?"

"I think I can squeeze him in during lunch, if that works with his schedule." The shuffle of paper and then pages being turned sounded from the background. Mary Margaret was old school with her calendar. "Yes, that will definitely work. And I'm excited to meet your grandfather. You talk about him a lot."

"He's a big part of my life. But about your schedule, if it's an inconvenience, you don't need to see him today. Brad's not going anywhere." Visions of comforting Gramps after another failed effort to contact Brad floated through my head, so procrastination wasn't feeling like a terrible thing.

"No problem. I have a long lunch today. It actually works out well for me."

And that doctor's appointment wasn't going to go away.

"Right," I mumbled. "Today it is. I'll make sure he's home. I have a client appointment and can't attend, but that might work out best anyway. That way, you can be vague, tell him you're writing up a report for me since I'm the paying client, and then I can break the bad news to him later."

Gramps' disappointment, psych appointments, my conniving aunt and uncle. Blech. Too many yucky things all converging in too narrow a time frame. It was like I had a cosmic black mark on my calendar for the week.

I popped a second donut in the toaster oven. Today was looking like a two-donut day.

"Oh, goodness." Mary Margaret sighed. "I suppose he will be terribly upset. I guess that's as good a way to handle it as any other."

"Thank you, Mary Margaret." As soon as she hung up, I grabbed the third and final donut from my freezer.

Yeah, this was gonna be a three-donut day for sure.

What had Beth told me? Something about me

tipping over the edge and starting to see Brad if I didn't hurry up and eat some Cheetos?

Donuts would have to do.

7
HILLARY

My phone rang just as I was finishing up with my lunch client, a successful businesswoman who didn't have the time or patience to keep up with styles or find outfits that fit and flattered her particular body type.

Getting paid to shop was the bomb. I loved my job. Okay, I loved all of my jobs, hence my current life dilemma.

But that was a worry for another time. I tapped the ignore button and quickly wrapped up the session.

My phone rang again as I walked to my car, and this time I stopped to see who was calling. I had two missed calls, both from Mary Margaret, and she was the one ringing me now. Oh, banana fudge fingers. That was not good.

I answered as I got into my car. "What's happened? Did Gramps freak out? Is he okay?" When she didn't answer right away, I said, "Are *you* okay?"

Mary Margaret's voice came across thin and reedy. "Your grandfather is fine. I, however, am not. Can you come right now?"

The stones of my cat-eye sunglasses bit into my hand. I didn't even remember pulling them from my purse. I slipped them on, chucked my purse into the passenger seat, and asked, "What's happened?"

"Ahh. I'm not sure. Maybe, um—"

"No, never mind. I'm driving, quick as I can. See you in ten." I hung up the phone, and then did my best to break every speed limit as safely as possible. Mary Margaret was unflappable... normally. This was *no bueno*. Also, I really needed to learn more Spanish. I lived in Texas, for goodness' sake.

By the time I arrived at Gramps', my heart was tap-dancing in my chest. It wasn't a pleasant feeling. Not at all.

On the drive, I'd managed no fewer than five horrifying scenarios, all extremely unlikely because they involved Gramps sick or injured, and *that* Mary Margaret would have told me immediately. Also, she'd specifically said that Gramps was fine.

After slamming my car door, I raced up the

driveway as fast as my three-inch heels allowed. Don't judge. I carried flats for dog walking.

Gramps came out of the house to meet me. "Slow down, Hillary. Everything's fine. I gave your friend a whiskey, and she's doing much better now."

He looked fine. No, better than fine. He looked tickled pink.

Wait, whiskey? Mary Margaret wasn't much of a drinker, so exactly how bad was this situation? At least it wasn't 911 bad. Uh-oh. "You didn't call 911, did you?"

"Pshaw. No." Even as he dismissed my question, Gramps had a certain twinkle in his eye I didn't particularly like.

I wasn't worried anyone was bleeding...but something was up. "What did you do to Mary Margaret, Gramps? She's a nice woman."

"She's a peach. And good at her job. This one's a keeper, peanut." He paused, beaming at me, then said, "She can see Brad."

Riiight.

I grabbed Gramps by the arm and pulled him the rest of the way up the walk, my heels making a satisfying click on the pavement as I approached the house.

"Hey, now. Don't get yourself in a state. I'm coming."

"Too late. I'm already in a state. You broke my

psychic. Of course I'm upset." I followed Gramps, who'd taken the lead to open the back door, into the kitchen.

I found Mary Margaret sitting at the kitchen table. She looked a little pale and had a whiskey glass in front of her, but otherwise seemed fine. And she was busily texting on her phone. That had to be good sign. Probably. People in shock didn't text, did they?

Since she was otherwise occupied, I addressed her companion at the table, a hot guy who was quietly observing us all. "I'm sorry—who are you? And why are you here?"

And since when did Gramps start hanging out with men who looked yummy enough to take home and lock in my basement? If I had a basement...and was a creepy sex fiend who locked up hot men in my basement. Clearly, I was befuddled by his buff biceps, broad shoulders, tousled, dark hair, pretty blue eyes, and overall aw-shucks hotness. He was like Clark Kent without the glasses. I really had a thing for Clark Kent.

"Ha!" Gramps cackled. "I knew it!"

His enthusiastic hollering had me shelving my dirty thoughts for the moment.

Then I realized that the strange man was eyeing me with a ridiculous degree of surprise. Finally, he said, "You can see me?" His piercing gaze met mine. "You can see me."

My heart thudded to a stop.

Okay, probably not, but it sure as heck felt like it, because everything inside me froze and felt tight, like a giant was squeezing me in his big fist.

I might be having a panic attack. Or something.

Probably I was losing my bananas.

Because if I wasn't mistaken, I was meeting...Brad.

I was seeing a figment of my grandfather's imagination. If that wasn't me going bananas, then...well, I didn't know what it was. And here was me not knowing that hallucinations were contagious.

I rubbed my eyes under my sunglasses, then realized I'd likely smeared my mascara and eyeliner. I closed my eyes but kept the glasses on. Brad might be a construct of my grandfather's wild imagination, but if he wasn't—if he was a real guy—then he was a serious hottie. No girl wanted to look like a psychotic raccoon when meeting an attractive man, even if that attractive man wasn't real.

Yeah, none of that made sense. Nifty. I was seeing things *and* my brain had turned to mush.

When I finally opened my eyes, Mr. Imaginary Hot Guy was still there. Except now he was standing and pointing at me.

"She can see me." He looked at Gramps with a

ridiculously large grin spreading across his face—and really, how was it possible he could look hotter? But he did.

I couldn't believe the words I was about to utter, but... "I guess you're Brad."

At his slow nod, I sank into the chair next to Mary Margaret.

She'd stopped texting and was watching Brad and me with great interest. "I've cancelled the rest of my appointments for the afternoon." Then she nudged her whiskey glass closer to me.

"Fabulous," I replied, then downed the remainder of her whiskey.

8
BRAD

Why wasn't everyone in the room as excited as me?

The way I saw it, Mary Margaret could miraculously see evidence of ghosts, which was a bonus talent for her, and Hillary should be thrilled that she finally had evidence Walter wasn't cracked.

I knew she worried about his mental health. Who wouldn't with a hallucination keeping him company twenty-four seven? And especially with his upcoming shrink visit.

But now she had proof I existed. Her grandfather wasn't seeing things, and he had a good friend rooming with him—not a hallucination. How was that not excellent news?

With any luck, the whiskey would soften up the

two women, because as it stood, both were looking pretty grim. As I waited and watched, Walter sat down at the table.

He rubbed his whiskery chin. "Haven't had this many visitors in a long time."

Hillary motioned for the whiskey bottle.

Walter raised an eyebrow but pushed the bottle toward her.

"Don't worry. I'm not driving." She poured a few fingers into the glass. "It's your fault, so you're giving me a ride home."

"How am I responsible? I've always been honest about Brad," Walter sniffed. "Well, after the first few months. I wasn't so sure myself in the beginning."

"Anyone else wondering why I'm suddenly visible? Hey." I nudged Walter. "Ask the expert."

Walter looked at Mary Margaret and said, "He wants to know how Hillary can see him."

Hillary's head ping-ponged between Mary Margaret and me. "I thought... Mary Margaret, if you can't see him—

"Or hear," I said.

Hillary glared at me then turned back to Mary Margaret. "If you can't see or hear him, how do you know he's there?"

"I can see his aura." Mary Margaret traced an outline of Brad's form in the air. The lines in her forehead deepened with concentration. "An impetuous nature, a generous soul, guilt..." Her finger stopped. "I shouldn't be able to see a dead man's aura." She turned toward Brad. "I'm sorry. I usually ask first."

"Tell her it's okay." I leaned my forearms on the table and studied the psychic with a nun's name.

Mary Margaret was absolutely the real deal.

She'd hit on my guilt, an emotion I'd been toting around for three years like so much excess but firmly attached baggage. I had no idea why I felt guilty. If I'd committed some horrible crime in my former life. If I'd left some important business unfinished. But the emotion was persistent in its presence, and Mary Margaret had spotted it.

If she could tell me what fed the uncomfortable (sometimes oppressive) emotion, I'd be grateful. Maybe then I could work my way through it. As it was, with my memory missing, the emotion was static.

Hillary repeated my comment to Mary Margaret, then said, "He also brought up a very important point: why can I see him, and why now?" She removed her sunglasses as she spoke, revealing smudged makeup underneath. When she glanced back at me, she did a double take and looked utterly baffled.

After a few seconds of blinking, followed by a

quick scan of the room, she put her sunglasses back on.

And that was when she made eye contact with me. Which made me wonder if—

"Holy bananas," Hillary said. "It's the glasses." She pulled the bridge of the glasses down her nose and peered at me over the top, then pushed them back into place. "Ohmigod, it *is* the glasses."

Mary Margaret held out her hand, and Hillary passed the gaudy specs to her.

She put the sunglasses on and repeated Hillary's procedure, pushing the glasses down the bridge of her nose and back up again. Then she did it again. "No, it's not working. I'm getting nothing."

"That can't be right." Hillary snatched the glasses back. As soon as she had them in place, she nodded. "They definitely work for me."

"Where did you get them?" I asked. "They look old."

"Vintage, not old," she replied automatically then shook her head. "Sorry, Every Woman's Fairy Godmother." My confusion must have been apparent, because she added, "Yes, I suppose you don't get out and about much, being…ah, ghostly and all. It's a popular vintage store in south Austin."

Even if I wasn't ghostly and did get out, I was fairly certain I wouldn't know that. Although who was I kidding? I had no idea what my habits had been prior to death, because I had no memory of them.

"The glasses are magic?" It sounded even funnier out loud than it had in my head.

Walter snorted. "And you had a hard time, peanut, believing Brad was real. *You're* the one with the magic glasses."

"Hey, Gramps, give me a break. I didn't know they were magic."

"We're not sure they *are* magic," Mary Margaret said. "What's magic, anyway, but science we can't yet explain?"

Said the psychic, which made it a little bit funny.

Mary Margaret wasn't anything like I'd expected. She'd shown up dressed more like a librarian than a psychic...assuming psychics dressed a certain way. I'd have thought bright colors and gauzy fabrics, if anyone had asked before today. Now, I wasn't so sure.

She was short, trim, and had to be at least midfifties. Her hair was silver and her makeup the kind that made you realize she was probably wearing some, because she looked great but it wasn't otherwise noticeable.

In short, Mary Margaret looked like she'd be comfortable on a tennis court, playing a hand of bridge, or baking cookies. She didn't look like someone who read auras or saw ghosts.

All of which meant that I needed to get out more.

I'd missed part of a discussion concerning the source of the glasses' magic, but some of the theories they were spouting now seemed silly.

So silly that I didn't mind throwing my own out there. I cleared my throat, which caught Walter and Hillary's attention. "Every Woman's Fairy Godmother?"

"Right," Hillary said. "That's where I got them."

I raised my eyebrows. "And who's the fairy godmother at Every Woman's Fairy Godmother?"

Hillary laughed. "Ah, no. Madeleine? I don't think Madeleine is secretly practicing witchcraft on the side."

"Who said she was a witch?" I shrugged. "Maybe she's your fairy godmother—just like the name of the store says."

"That's a marketing gimmick." Hillary peered at me, and I couldn't help but find it annoying that she could only make eye contact with me when her eyes were shaded by tinted spectacles. "Kind of like: we have everything you could possibly desire; come shop here."

"Wait a minute now, sweet pea. Don't be so hasty to discount it."

"I agree with Walter and Brad." Mary Margaret glanced between Walter and Hillary. "What? Like I can't read between the lines? Just because I can't hear Brad, doesn't mean his suggestion is wrong."

While that statement made little sense, I wasn't going to argue with a woman who was on my side. "Right, so you check out the Madeleine woman."

Hillary's eyebrows pulled together, giving her a fierce (though somehow simultaneously cute) expression. "Or I could just ask her where the store's name comes from." Her expression turned thoughtful. "Sure, I can do that. That's completely innocuous. Anyone might ask that. You guys have to remember that I do a ton of business with this woman. I *do not* need her thinking I'm a complete loon."

"Fair enough," Mary Margaret said.

"Shelved until you can have a talk with your saleslady," Walter said. "But you might think of a backup plan if she gives a generic, vague answer."

"Fine," Hillary agreed. "What about this aura business? If Brad's dead, how does he have one?"

Mary Margaret rubbed her collarbone. "Ah, about that... Dead people don't have auras. Not in my experience."

Then she looked at me—more specifically, my aura—and frowned.

Wait, what? Dead people don't have auras, so...I wasn't dead?

The heart that I didn't physically have started to thud at an alarming rate.

Mary Margaret couldn't hear me, so I was

thankful Hillary spoke on my behalf. "If Brad's not dead, then he's not a ghost. What is he?"

Mary Margaret looked at me (my aura) with kindness in her eyes, then said to Hillary, "Other than a man with a generous soul, which I think you already knew, I can't tell you."

Mary Margaret thought I had a generous soul? Wow, that definitely did not match up with the guilt I'd been carrying around for the last three years.

Hillary turned her scowl on me. "What are you?"

As if I had any more answers than she did.

Thankfully, Walter came to my rescue, because explaining to a gorgeous woman that I didn't know *who* I was, let alone *what* I was, was about as emasculating as it sounded.

"Brad isn't his real name. When we met three years ago, he didn't have any memory of who he was. I found out later that he'd been living in an empty house a few doors down."

"When they tore it down a few weeks later, that's when I moved in." No point in explaining that I could have easily found another place to haunt.

I'd moved in because Walter had needed me as much as I'd needed him. It was pretty awesome that a human being could see and speak to me. Even better that the human was Walter, an amazing guy and exceptional company, even given the age gap between us. But the best part had been that I'd been able to pay him back for his desperately needed companionship with a little nudge toward a better life. I hated to think back on how bad a shape my friend had been in all those years ago.

Walter flashed a sad smile at me. "Let me tell it, son, so Mary Margaret gets it the first time round."

I nodded.

"So, I'm looking less than my best, wearing a robe twenty-four seven, needing a haircut, and this guy"—Walter hitches a thumb in my direction—"sees me fetching my mail one day. He's standing in my yard, and I say, 'Get off my lawn,' or something similar, and after that, I couldn't shake him. I was the first person who'd spoken to him in months. Since he'd died, we thought. But now, who knows?"

"What could you be?" Hillary's eyes filled with sympathy. "Are you undead or half dead or, I don't know, cursed?"

A nasty chill crawled up my back. "How would I know if I was cursed?"

Walter repeated the question for Mary Margaret. Her eyes got big. "I don't do curses. I don't do anything that alters someone's reality. I just read what's already there."

"But do you know other psychics that would know about"—Walter frowned, his bushy eyebrows bunching together—"people who are dead but not really dead? Or curses and such like? Not that Madame Celeste. She was a fraud."

Mary Margaret refrained from commenting on Madame Celeste's talent or lack thereof, but she did pinch her lips together. I knew that look. That was an "if you don't have something nice to say, say nothing at all" expression.

Although where—or rather who—I knew it from, I couldn't say.

"I do have a small network, mostly online, of people I trust. They all have some connection to the supernatural. I can start by asking if anyone else has experience with someone who's dead but not dead." Mary Margaret nodded in my direction. "Apologies. Until we find a word for what you are..."

I shrugged. I appreciated everyone's help. I didn't realize there might be actual answers to the questions Walter and I had thrown around over the years. That Mary Margaret and Hillary were willing to help me find them was outstanding news. The very best, in fact.

"He's fine with whatever you want to call him. Is anyone else wondering at the timing of all this? The suspicious, perhaps auspicious, timing of Brad's discovery?" Walter asked. "Remember, peanut? My appointment with the psych doctor lady."

Hillary's head slowly fell forward until her forehead touched the kitchen table. And then she started to bang her head—not *too* hard—on the wooden surface.

"Should you maybe stop her?" I asked Walter. But Walter just shook his head.

Finally, she stopped, but her head remained firmly planted on the table. "How am I related to those terrible people?"

"They're not terrible, just confused and concerned," Walter said.

A mumble emerged from under the thick red waves that had fallen to cover her face.

"What was that?" I asked.

Hillary lifted her head up off the table. A red mark marred the skin on her forehead.

"I said they're greedy." She shoved the bridge of her glasses with her finger. "Okay. Here's what we do." She pointed at me. "You're dead or not quite dead, so we find out exactly what's going on with you and how to fix you. If you're Gramps' living, in-the-flesh boarder, he's not crazy, so we make you visible and preferably touchable." Her cheeks pinked and she quickly turned to Mary Margaret. "Your job is to milk your network for clues as to whatever Brad might be. Find out if he's fixable. Or, if not, what we do with him."

"Whoa. What you do with me?" That didn't sound good. Not at all.

She chewed her bottom lip, a good sign that

what was about to come wouldn't be good. "Gramps might lose his house and end up in an assisted living facility because of his relationship with you. We'll try to fix your problem, but if we can't... Well, Gramps' situation is pretty dire. You've lived with him for three years. You *know* he can't lie to save his life. So we make you visible to the general populace—in particular, one psychiatrist—or we need to find another solution, one where you're not living here."

"Wait a minute, peanut. You can't kick Brad out. This is his home." Walter looked a little ashamed of his granddaughter.

But he shouldn't be. I got it. Like she said, I'd been Walter's roommate—his friend—for three years. I'd helped him by being here, but times had changed. If leaving helped him now, then I'd leave.

Unless the two highly motivated women sitting across the kitchen table found a way to make me flesh again.

Please, please let that happen.

Please let Mary Margaret and her aura-reading skills not be wrong.

Please let me still be alive.

9
HILLARY

Scenery flew by as I stared out the passenger window. I should feel bad. I *did* feel bad.

Gramps had been a mess after Gran died. *Ugh.* That robe. He'd worn this tatty old robe over his PJs, and try as I might, I couldn't convince him that dressing every day—even if he wasn't leaving the house—was important for his mental health.

But Brad had.

Brad, who was real.

Mostly real.

And more than getting rid of the biggest fashion crime of the century, Brad had gotten Gramps moving, gotten him eating. Heck, Gramps was healthier now than he'd been before Gran died. He was all "organic" this and "my heart rate" that. The guy wore a fitness tracker and shopped at Whole Foods. So much better than the high-sodium, processed- and canned-food-heavy diet he'd previously preferred.

Because of Brad.

And I'd told him we might be kicking him to the curb.

Uh-huh. It was possible I was a terrible human being.

"Quit beating yourself up." Gramps looked at me, but only briefly. He took driving seriously. He was that kind of guy. He signaled, he stopped fully at stop signs, and he drove the speed limit.

"I basically told the guy he was a second-class citizen."

Gramps snorted. "He doesn't have a physical body and most people can't see him. I'm not sure that's entirely incorrect. Besides, he gets it. You're trying to protect me. You two share that particular trait, an oversized do-gooder gene."

I rolled my eyes. Because really? I wasn't a do-gooder just because I wanted one of the people I loved most in this world to be treated fairly...by his own darn family.

"And you got all that information from him," Gramps reminded me. "So maybe you can dig up some good information on his past."

True. Before we left, I'd jotted down everything

Gramps and Brad knew about Brad's past and his circumstances before he started rooming with my grandfather. Maybe digging into his history would reveal something about his present circumstances.

My notes were shockingly thin. Having a case of amnesia would do that, I supposed.

While I dug around trying to find some connection between ghostly Brad and a live human being with a past and maybe even a family, Mary Margaret would be tapping into her network of professional resources in an attempt to discover *what* he was. The hope was that we'd be able to address his lack of physical substance if we knew what he was or how he came to be ghostlike.

And we were doing all of this because Brad was real.

"I'm still trying to wrap my head around Brad. The fact that he's actually living in your house. I always thought he was a kind of bootstrapping mechanism. A way for you to yank yourself out of...uh—"

"The depression I sank into after your gran died? You can say it. I was depressed." He checked his blind spot, signaled a lane change, then smoothly slid into the next lane. "I know exactly how poorly I was doing. I have a record."

"I don't understand."

"Brad arm-twisted me into keeping a journal of

all my daily activities, including showering, shaving, eating, that kind of thing. It's pretty damn depressing reading it, let alone remembering living it."

"I didn't know that."

He shrugged. "That's how he convinced me to start making some changes. I'm just lucky I wasn't to the point of needing medical intervention. Having a friend threaten to scare the pants off me in the middle of the night was enough for me to at least keep the journal. I'm lucky that recording my miserable state woke me up, and that having a companion to walk with and someone to keep me company during meals made a difference. I know that wouldn't work for a lot of folks."

Wow. I knew Brad had made an impact in Gramps life, but...wow. "We'll fix him."

He raised his eyebrows but kept his eyes on the road. "Fix him?"

"You know, make him...himself again."

"If that's possible. I hope for his sake it is. But you should do it for his sake, not mine. No one deserves to live like he has for the last few years."

"I'm doing it for both of you." And that was the absolute truth. I needed Gramps free of my aunt and uncle's machinations, but I also wanted the man who'd made such an amazing impact on Gramps' life to have a life of his own.

"You drive too fast." I was completely full of it,

but I felt compelled to say it, since he always gave me grief about how fast *I* drove. (I didn't. I drove with the flow of traffic.)

Gramps laughed. "I don't, and you know it."

Silence fell again. We'd almost arrived home before Gramps spoke again.

"Whatever you and Mary Margaret do to help Brad, be careful. He deserves a chance to be whole again. But..." He rubbed his jaw, and the sandpaper sound of fingers on stubble made me turn to him. "But if Mary Margaret is wrong and Brad *is* dead, you can't send him on his way, metaphysically speaking. You can't send him to the afterlife. He's not ready."

I let out a huge breath. This was big stuff. Mary Margaret, Gramps, and I were about to stick our noses into something we couldn't even begin to understand.

"I know I mentioned it before and you weren't keen, but...there's another option if we can't get his body back."

Gramps gripped the wheel harder.

My chest tightened uncomfortably, but we really should talk about alternatives. We needed a Plan B, even if Plan B sucked. "He could move away."

Gramps scowled as he turned into my neighborhood. "It's his home, peanut. He's lived there three years, and he doesn't know anything else. The man has no contact with other people outside of me, and now you when you're wearing those glasses. That's no way for a human being to live. No, he can't 'move away,' Hillary."

I didn't state the obvious: that we weren't entirely sure Brad was human at all.

"I'm just talking about a Plan B here, Gramps." He arched a judgmental eyebrow, so I made the point that needed to be made. "Carol and Tim aren't going to be reasonable, not when one keeps cheering the other on. They're like a starving dog with a meaty bone. How did such a nice man have such terrible children?"

"Be kind, peanut. They're worried." After a brief pause, he added, "And they're good kids."

That hesitation spoke volumes, but it would take more than the threat of commitment to a facility for Gramps to openly admit that his children were anything less than his idealized versions of themselves.

Gramps was a really, really good guy, sometimes to a fault.

"*Are* they worried, Gramps? Are they really? How often do they come to check on you? How much time do they spend with you?" I bit my lip. They were his children, but my sweet-tempered, big-hearted grandfather needed a reality check. "They may have started out concerned, but now all they can see is how much easier everyone's lives would be if your house was sold and you were living under supervision."

He wrinkled his nose when I mentioned supervision, and well he should. He wasn't ten. Even so, he still defended them.

As he pulled into my drive and parked, I had to listen to him tell me how busy they both were with their demanding jobs (because apparently my four businesses were a piece of cake to run), and how Tim was newly married and had recently moved (yeah, and?), and how Carol was busy with her own children (who also didn't visit very often).

But I held my tongue through all of his excuses.

Finally, he said, "And, peanut, it is just a house."

I looked at him, truly looked at him. I let myself see the lines and the wrinkles and the sun spots and the ear hair and the receding hairline—all the things that were normally faded or washed away by my love for him.

Yes, he was getting older. And yes, he looked a little tired around his eyes. But he was still fit, active, sharp, and very capable of taking care of himself. The man cooked for me, not the other way around, when I came to dinner. He had cleaners, but he did all the tidying himself, and his laundry, as well. The house was terribly dated, but it was in good shape.

Long story short, he was doing great in the house that he'd lived in and loved for over fifty years.

"Is it just a house to you? Because if that's true... If that's true, we can sell it quickly and set you up in a place that you choose." I didn't mention it, but a place with enough room for Brad, as well.

"If it comes to selling, I'd rather decide where to live than have the choice taken away. Of course I would. But for now, I want to do what I can to stay. Brad and I are comfortable there." He fell silent. "Almost all of my memories of your grandmother are tied together with that house."

Gramps was a stand-up guy and wouldn't ever want to hurt someone to benefit himself, but also—I'd now met Brad.

Brad was good people, too.

I'd heard the stories for years, but meeting him solidified all of those stories into a (mostly) real person.

A yummy, dark-haired person with well-defined arms and a charming dimple.

Too bad Brad wasn't one hundred percent alive and human, because he was certainly one hundred percent hot.

"Peanut?"

"Hm?" I blinked, then realized we'd been parked and silent for several seconds. Gramps was looking at me with concern, probably wondering why the heck I hadn't gotten out of his truck yet.

"Get some sleep. You seem like you need it. Oh, and maybe think about selling off one of the businesses? You work too hard."

Except the glazed look in my eye hadn't been caused by overwork. It also wasn't a result of Gramps' looming psych eval and housing dilemma or the shock of discovering Gramps' imaginary friend was no figment of his imagination.

Nope.

It was the direct result of lusting after a guy who didn't exist as a physical person on this earth.

10

HILLARY

Good friends and clients made the world an easier place to live in.

I'd called in a few favors to have my errand running covered for the next few days. I'd also extended the few personal shopping deadlines that loomed over the next few days. And Beth was more than happy to pick up the dog walking, though explaining to her *why* I needed the help was a little tricky.

Let's just say ghosts, the dead and undead, and curses never came up, so I felt like a big Liar McLiarson.

But on the bright side, I had amazing clients. I needed to handle my personal shopping clients myself, but my errand and dog-walking clients trusted me to choose capable replacements to handle their requests and their dogs.

Which left me at home with my slim notes on Brad's background and an itch to learn more.

If only Brad could "remember" more of his former life. He seemed to experience brief flashes of familiarity, and he assumed those were memories of his former life.

So I was trying to make headway with snippets of information (a preference for whiskey on the rocks) that might not even be actual memories.

Nothing on the page jumped out at me. But maybe—I skimmed the list for the umpteenth time —just maybe, Brad's knowledge of a local high school's mascot meant he attended that high school.

Or not, because I knew several mascots for several local high schools, not one of them mine. Professional errand runner here. It came up in my work.

But maybe, just maybe, Brad's mascot knowledge was important, so it was time for some research.

Two hours later, after trawling through so many internet sites that my clicking finger had started to ache, I found...something.

Search for Stephen Bradley Sherwood, missing man, suspended.

The article had popped up on page six of my search results when I'd entered the local high school and the name Brad, because—shockingly—I couldn't find a roster of high school students from the high school in question. I guessed that kind of thing wasn't published on the internet.

The article was dated three years ago.

A shiver of foreboding crawled up my spine.

I scrolled through the article, then steeled myself to read it more closely a second time.

The authorities had called off the search after two days when they discovered the date of Stephen Sherwood's disappearance was the first anniversary of his girlfriend's death in a tragic car accident. Suicide was suspected, but no body was found.

Suicide. A tragic accident. His girlfriend dead.

I kept reading.

The article didn't contain a picture but did mention that Stephen had gone missing from his mother's home in Austin and that he'd been living in Minnesota for several months prior to his death.

I double-checked the date of the article. Three years ago—more specifically, a few months before Walter ran into Brad on his lawn.

Stephen Bradley Sherwood had been twenty-six at the time of his disappearance. Brad could pass for twenty-six, though I would have guessed a little older. That might be because his behavior was so... adult? Not that twenty-six-year-old men weren't adults, but...yeah, they weren't like Brad.

As for the name? If Brad actually was Stephen Bradley Sherwood, that would be downright spooky. I'd have to ask Gramps how he'd landed on Brad, because I understood that Gramps had come up with the name when the man on his lawn couldn't produce one of his own.

It was too soon to say if Stephen Sherwood was Brad, but the timeline of Sherwood's disappearance certainly seemed to line up with the appearance of Brad.

What I needed now was to verify that Stephen Bradley Sherwood had never been discovered, alive or dead.

And if he hadn't? Then I needed a picture.

Actually, with a full name and the magic of the internet, a picture might be the fastest way to resolve this mystery.

This terrible mystery that involved a dead woman and a possible suicide.

A picture of Stephen Sherwood became my first priority.

But then a twinge in my back started to inch toward more of an ache, and I decided that Sherwood's picture could wait until after I'd stretched.

Because stretching was really important. Didn't want to get a hinky back or anything.

Or confirm that Brad was Stephen Sherwood, a

man who'd been involved in the tragic death of his girlfriend and might possibly have killed himself.

Yep, stretching was good.

I went through a series of stretches that I used when writing for my blog consumed me and I sat for too long, but when I was done, I realized I desperately needed to eat something. I'd had whiskey for lunch—never a brilliant idea—and on top of that had missed dinner.

Food was really important. If I was hungry, I wouldn't make good decisions, right?

Right.

One sandwich and a handful of Cheetos later, I returned to my computer to find an instant message from Mary Margaret.

The tension that had gathered in my neck eased. I definitely had to read this first, before I did any kind of search for a picture. She could have found vital information.

What she'd found was confirmation from three different sources that an aura meant alive in some sense of the word.

I sent a video chat invite, and Mary Margaret popped up on my screen. I wasn't procrastinating. Not at all.

"Hey. What else did you find?" (I was totally procrastinating.)

Mary Margaret tucked a few strands of silver hair

behind her ear. "A general consensus that if you've got an aura, you're alive. But apparently the undead also have an aura—a very distinctive one."

Undead? What kind of world was I living in? A different one than I'd known just a day ago.

"Please tell me Brad isn't among the undead. I'm not even sure what that means, but it sounds just about as permanent as dead." I tipped my laptop screen back, so I could lean back in my chair.

"The undead angle is highly unlikely. One of my contacts has seen the aura of an undead. She said it was unmistakably different, and I couldn't miss it."

"So, according to your people, Brad's neither dead nor undead, which leaves...?"

Mary Margaret frowned. "Alive but invisible?"

"Hm. I don't know. I don't suppose you touched his...uh, his aura?" Why did that sound so dirty?

Mary Margaret chuckled. "No, I did not grope that young man's personal energy. Why do you ask?"

"Just a random thought. He was sitting in a chair." Mary Margaret shook her head, so I elaborated. "He wasn't falling through the chair, so I'm wondering if he has some substance. I should have touched him when I had the chance."

And there I went again with the pervy, creepy vibe.

Mary Margaret leaned closer to her screen. "You're blushing."

I glared.

"Fine, we won't talk about it. But you should ask Walter if he's had any physical contact with Brad. They've lived together for three years. He should know if Brad has any substance."

"I'll do that when we're done. It's weird that I didn't notice immediately—maybe because I saw a man in the kitchen and just assumed he was a normal guy?—but Brad doesn't look like everyone else. His edges are fuzzy."

"Fuzzy edges?"

"Right. That sounds nutty, doesn't it? You know what, never mind, because how is talking about my grandfather's imaginary friend come to life going to sound but nutty?"

Mary Margaret laughed, and she didn't do it in that "you're so crazy I want you to think I'm laughing with but I'm just really worried" way.

She swallowed the last of her mirth and said, "Find out if Brad can interact with objects. Maybe that will spark some new discussion on my end. Although I wouldn't expect much. While we've all had our share of run-ins with the truly bizarre, we have limited expertise in, well, things like Brad. We mostly talk about breaking bad news, helping clients through grief, when to refer to a counselor, that sort of thing."

"I'll definitely find out if Brad can interact at all

with physical things." I peered at Mary Margaret. She had a certain look about her... "What aren't you saying?"

She frowned. "Have you considered an expert? Someone like a paranormal investigator?"

Yuck. Just no. It had taken me ages to find Mary Margaret. After the Madame Celeste incident, I was leery to try just anyone that claimed psychic ability.

"Please tell me you have someone in mind, because other than you, my last few experiences with psychics haven't been stellar."

"First, I read auras. I'm not a psychic." But that response was an automatic one. I could tell she was thinking about my question. "I seem to recall someone, but I can't remember the particulars. I'll touch base with my network. Even if they don't have anyone local, a good investigator should be able to make a local referral, right?"

"Maybe."

"Have you talked to the shop owner?"

I blinked guiltily back at her. Why had we opted for video chat instead of a phone call? Oh, right, that had been me. I'd done that. After squirming in my chair, I replied, "No, I haven't called Madeleine. I'm sure she's got nothing to do with this, and I really don't want to upset her. Her store is amazing, and I really like shopping there."

That last part might have sounded a little whiney.

"Quit whining. Call Madeleine."

Before I could protest or offer any argument at all as to why that was a terrible idea, she ended the chat.

As the window closed, my screen was filled once again with the article about the missing man.

"Dang it. How could I forget to tell her about my lead?" My depressing, disturbing lead.

"Tell who about what lead?"

"Aaagh!" My reflexive flinch made my chair roll. I was perched precariously on the edge of my seat, so the unexpected movement deposited me on the floor. "Ow, ow, ow, ow, ow, ow."

Brad, with his rumpled, dark hair and his Clark Kent aw-shucks, cute-hot look, stood about ten feet away. He did look sorry, to give him a little credit.

"I tried to knock." He demonstrated by rapping his knuckles against the wall. While his hand appeared to make contact, no sound resulted.

"How did you get here?" But then I realized I was inside. Inside and working on my computer. I practically smacked my face in my haste to check for sunglasses that I knew weren't there.

"Where are your sparkly shades?" Brad looked about as confused as I felt...except he was standing, not sprawled in an inelegant heap on the floor.

I scrambled to my feet and resisted the temptation to rub my tailbone. "Not on my face, so how am I seeing you?"

He shook his head.

"Right. Of course you don't know. You don't even know how the glasses made you visible to begin with. Or how you became invisible or ghostly or whatever you are. Heck, you don't even know *what* you are."

"I'd like to." His voice was small, and that was a change. The Brad I'd met in Gramps' kitchen earlier today had spoken with an easy assurance. He hadn't been obnoxiously loud or overly assertive, but nothing about him had been small or quiet.

I considered my words and cringed. Now *I* was the one who needed to apologize. "I didn't mean it the way it sounded. Not at all. Uh, so how did you get here?"

"I walked and took the bus."

"Really?" I was pretty sure my eyes were bugging out. "The bus?"

He shrugged.

"Right." He took the bus...because that was what ghost types did. They used public transport. I couldn't think of what to say, because...the bus?

"I can't drive, and even if I could, Walter loves his truck. I don't think he'd give me the keys."

Someone had a better sense of humor about this

situation than me, and that someone had been stuck with no sense of touch, no physical human contact for three years.

"Cool, so the bus. Yeah, that's cool. Uh—"

"You have a lead?"

Thank you, Brad, for saving me from my awkward self, except my lead kinda sucked. "I do. Does the name Stephen Bradley Sherwood mean anything?"

As soon as the name left my lips, all hell broke loose.

11

BRAD

Hearing the name "Stephen Bradley," elicited a chill, but then Hillary said "Sherwood" and my gut started to burn.

I had no true memory of physical pain. An advantage to my memory loss I hadn't recognized until this very moment.

Certainly, I knew I'd felt pain as a human, and I retained a general understanding of what it meant to experience it. But this—

"Oh, no. No. You don't look so good." All the color washed away from Hillary's face.

"Don't feel great."

"You're flickering. Should you be flickering?" Her thick red hair whipped around her face. "Why is there wind in my living room? Brad? Are you okay?"

It was a ridiculous question. Something to say in the midst of a crisis. Because no, no, I wasn't okay.

My gut wrenched again, and this time my body was wrapped in a burning, bone-chilling cold. If my body could be turned inside out like a dirty sock, then it was happening now.

Pain sucked.

Not feeling pain, that half-life I'd been living and complaining about up until a few seconds ago, maybe wasn't so bad. Who needed a fully physical, pain-feeling body?

It hurt, and it wouldn't stop. Was I dying? Was this what it felt like to die when you weren't really, fully alive?

But then the pain did stop. It didn't ease and lessen. It came to a complete, stutter-free halt.

I took stock.

No pain. Thank the heavens for that. I was back to not feeling at all, but I'd take it over the excruciating burning awfulness of what I'd just experienced. The twisting horror of my insides becoming my outsides was an experience I'd gladly leave behind.

No wind. There'd been gusts of wind in the middle of Hillary's living room. But it was still now.

Maybe because I wasn't in Hillary's living room any longer.

There was no living room, and there was no Hillary.

I was in a completely different location—clothing store?

"Oh, good. Nice to see you still in one piece." A woman with brown hair stood a few feet away. She was pretty enough but not vibrantly gorgeous like Hillary.

"Who are you? And where am I?"

"I'm Madeleine."

That name sounded familiar, but given the obscene cold, the vicious burning, the inside-out twisting, and the disappearance of both Hillary and her living room, I wasn't exactly at my sharpest.

"Hillary's mentioned me, perhaps? Every Woman's Fairy Godmother?"

And then several pieces snapped together in my mind. "The vintage store." I looked around again and realized I was quite likely inside that very shop. "The glasses." I examined her. She looked normal enough, and yet... "You can see me."

"Well, yes, I can. It's a perk of the profession."

"I don't suppose you're referring to your shop-owning career." I crossed my arms. This lady better start spilling, or I'd...I'd... I'd do absolutely nothing, because I had no physical body, and even if I did, what was I going to do? Put her in a headlock?

"I'm not supposed to say, but given the circumstances..." She bit her lip and wrinkled her nose in what might be a cutely indecisive way under different circumstances. As it was, I found her hesitance annoying.

Actually, nerve-racking might be more accurate.

"Right. I can tell *you*. *You're* cursed. You're not a normal, run-of-the-mill, magic-unaffected human, so I'm sure it's fine. It's not really breaking a rule, more like bending it. Right?" She looked at me like I had some clue how to answer that question.

Like I had some clue what she was talking about in general.

But mostly I just heard *magic* and *cursed*. "I'm cursed?"

Her mouth formed into an O, then she pursed her lips and tilted her head.

"You just magicked me to your shop. I'm running around in a nonexistent body and invisible to almost everyone. Lady, the cat's already halfway out of the bag. Now spill."

"I'm a fairy godmother."

I knew the name of the shop. I knew some weird, supernatural, paranormal, magic voodoo *something* was happening. I'd even hypothesized at some point that Hillary's favorite shop owner might be the very thing her shop proclaimed her to be. And yet... "A fairy godmother?"

"Don't sound so shocked. People are all about witches and werewolves and vampires these days. What happened to the fairy godmother love?" If I wasn't mistaken, someone was about to hop on her soapbox. "We're basically the cool cousin of witches, but more altruistic and with better magic. And we don't drink blood or go all furry and get infested with fleas. How are we not showing up in prime time?"

She looked like she wanted an actual answer, so I said, "Disney?"

Which was clearly the wrong answer, because she scowled. "Do you see me sporting wings? Or a poufy pastel dress in very poor taste? I own a vintage clothing store. I have excellent taste."

"Apologies. You asked about the prime-time thing, and I was just hypothesizing—"

"Never mind. I get a little carried away."

Yeah. Just a little, but commenting was in the realm of "do these jeans make my butt look big?" "No" means she doesn't have a nice rear, and "yes" means she's fat—which, of course, is not what any regular kinda guy means when he answers.

Apparently, I had some experience with women in my forgotten past, because I hadn't picked up that tidbit while living with Walter.

I didn't nod or shake my head, and I sure as heck didn't offer a verbal response. Silence could be a good interrogation tactic, so I waited in silence for her to cough up some information.

"You didn't know you were cursed?"

I shook my head.

"Um, surprise! You're cursed." And she made jazz hands, like she was giving me the good kind of surprise.

Maybe she was? Because if I was cursed... "I'm not dead."

"Definitely not dead." She held out her hand. "Sorry, I didn't catch your name."

She knew I was cursed, but not my name. Well, okay then.

I tried to take her hand, expecting not to be able to touch her—because I couldn't touch anyone and hadn't been able to for three years—and made skin-to-skin contact. I was startled enough that it took me a second to remember that I was supposed to be introducing myself. "Stephen Bradley Sherwood."

I hadn't thought. I'd been distracted by the touch of another (sort of) human, and the words had simply come out of my mouth. But as I spoke them, my gut twisted. The weird, getting-turned-inside-out feeling I'd experienced when I'd been transported to Madeleine's shop.

The warm pressure of Madeleine's hand squeezing mine chased away the feeling.

"No, you don't, you nasty little curse." She had a

determined glint in her eye, one I appreciated, because I was about ninety percent sure she'd just kept me from some terrible fate.

"I'm not sure why I said that. I don't actually remember who I am. I go by Brad."

"Well, Stephen, Brad"—she shrugged—"whichever, at least that little display lets me know something about your curse."

Information. At last.

"Whoever cursed you didn't want you to remember your past, including your identity, and they put some nasty traps in place on the off chance you figured a way around the memory block. Come here." She opened her arms like she was going to hug me.

She seemed like a nice lady and all, but—

"I don't bite. Come here. I'm going to see what I can do with your curse. It's terribly inconvenient."

Terribly inconvenient? That wasn't how I'd put it, but if she could help me then I was all in. She at least seemed to have a clue about what was happening to me.

I stepped closer.

She didn't hug me; she placed her hands on my shoulders and looked into my eyes. It was uncomfortably intimate. I wanted to look away but couldn't.

After several uncomfortable seconds, her hands

fell away. Immediately, I stepped back, one step, then two.

She huffed. "I've done what I can. Recovering your memory is up to you, but you won't have to worry that every piece of information you discover is going to pull you into the great nothingness of purgatory."

I blinked, considered her words, then blinked again. "Wait, what?"

She patted my arm. "That's where you were headed when I sensed a disturbance in the force and intervened." She grinned. "You like that one? I try to keep up with cultural references."

Since she seemed awfully proud of herself, I didn't mention that *Star Wars* had been around for about forty years, so she wasn't exactly on the cutting edge. "But...wait, I'm not going to purgatory?" She nodded, so I asked, "And I can freely dig into my past without consequence?"

She nodded again, which was good, because I really wanted to know who I'd been. Had I been a terrible person? What kind of person got himself cursed?

"I'd start with Stephen Bradley Sherwood, if I were you. That name had you on a path straight to the horrible grey yuck of purgatory." She wrinkled her nose again; this time it seemed to be with distaste. "Someone really doesn't like you, Stephen-Brad."

I had an enemy out in the world who was angry enough to curse me. That was a thoroughly unpleasant sensation.

But then, I also had a fairy godmother.

Had Disney gotten it all wrong and fairy godmothers weren't in the personal protection biz? Best to ask.

"Isn't it your job as my fairy godmother to know who's out there trying to ruin my life?" I didn't even mention the fact that she might have actually, you know, *protected* me from those people.

"Oh, gosh, Stephen-Brad. I'm not *your* fairy godmother! I'm Hillary's." Then she gave me a critical up-down look that made me feel a little like a piece of meat. "And I'm thinking my wand might need a little tune-up if you're the result of my... Well, never mind that." She shook her head.

If I'm the result of what?

But I couldn't ask, because just as quickly as I'd been yanked from Hillary's living room—but much less painfully, thank goodness—I was returned.

12

BRAD

Relief washed over me. I was practically drowning in the emotion.

To be back in Hillary's living room, a place I might not be very familiar with but one I'd traveled to on my own two feet, was an immense relief.

Also, it wasn't purgatory. Extra points for that.

And even better, Hillary's house contained Hillary. A wild-haired, freaked-out Hillary, but any Hillary was better than no Hillary.

"Did you know you have a fairy godmother?"

She yanked at her hair, which explained why it was looking particularly disheveled. "Where were you?"

She seemed upset. Very upset. "It's kind of a long story." I narrowed my eyes and examined the tense lines of her face, covered in part by her sparkly cat-eyed shades. "Why are you wearing the glasses?"

She slipped them down her nose as she stared at me, then heaved out a huge sigh. With that breath, some of the tension left her. "Brad, you disappeared."

"Right. It's a really weird story. I met—" I stopped, because she'd dropped onto her sofa and was pressing her fingers into her temples. "Are you okay?"

She looked up and choked out a laugh. "Really? You disappear into thin air—something my grandfather says you've never done before—and you're asking me if I'm okay? No, I'm not great. I'm two seconds away from the tension headache to end all headaches. I thought you'd gone to the great beyond. Or wherever ghosts go when they're done being ghosts."

She covered her mouth and muttered something about bananas and fudge then retrieved her phone from her jeans pocket. "I'm texting Gramps to let him know you're fine."

I swallowed the smile that was about to bust out across my face.

She'd been worried about me.

It might sound terrible that I found her worry a little entertaining and completely endearing, but given the context, it was pretty awesome. I was the guy whose disappearance would solve all of her grandfather's problems. With me gone, Walter would pass his psych eval. Probably.

"I used to have a friend that no one can see, but he's gone now" might not be the best argument for competence, but it was better than "I have an imaginary friend sitting next to me. He says hi."

When she'd finished texting, she stared at her phone, waiting for a reply. She didn't have to wait long. I patted myself on the back for that one. Walter had learned how to be succinct via text, because his thumb-typing speed was like his driving speed, conservatively average at best.

When her attention turned back to me, I assured her I was good. "And very, very happy not to be in purgatory."

The little color remaining in Hillary's face drained away. "That could happen? You could go there?"

"No, not anymore." Which only seemed to increase her panic. In the hopes that the full story would calm whatever fears I'd inadvertently triggered, I relayed it as quickly as possible.

When I got to the cursed-not-dead part, she melted into her sofa. "Cursed is bad, but so, so much better than dead."

We agreed on that point.

When I wrapped it all up by informing her that

Madeleine was her fairy godmother, Hillary laughed. I'd waited till the end to reveal the identity of the woman and the shop. Since Hillary had a personal connection to Madeleine, I thought she might be upset by that revelation.

"Yeah, right."

"You think I'm kidding?" I'd been pacing as I retold my mini-adventure, but I stopped now and sat in the armchair kitty-corner to the sofa. "Getting sucked through some weird space vortex to arrive in a place across town is completely believable, but not that your favorite shop owner was responsible for it? Purgatory is believable, but not fairy godmothers?"

She blinked at me, and I couldn't help but notice how very blue her eyes were. I knew they were light, probably on some level knew they were blue. It wasn't like we'd just met. I'd seen more of her over the last three years than any other person except Walter. She visited her grandfather a few times a week; she was a really terrific granddaughter.

But I wasn't a creeper. And when a lady couldn't see you, you didn't stare. No ogling, no casual checkouts, no scoping of any variety. That was just plain old manners and decency.

Sitting across from her now, I felt like I was seeing her in a way I'd never been allowed to before. I still wasn't a normal guy, *but I wasn't dead*.

Nope, not dead, just a guy with a curse hanging over his head.

Right. I wasn't exactly available, and it would be good to remember that.

Even if the simple act of shaking Madeleine's hand had reminded me what it felt like to touch another person.

Even if that touch had sparked a desire so deep it ached, a desire to simply touch another human being.

Wonderful. Now I wanted things I hadn't allowed myself to want in a very long time: to run my hands through the mass of Hillary's bright curls, to trace my finger along her jaw, to follow the freckles along her collarbone and beyond.

To touch another human being.

To touch Hillary.

"Madeleine? Really? The woman who snatched you from the gates of purgatory, who told you you're cursed, was Madeleine?" Hillary wasn't looking for affirmation. She was processing. I could see it on her face, so I waited, and I shoved all that achy desire for human contact back in the dark closet it had been locked in for three years.

She clasped her hands in her lap and stared at them for a while. Eventually, she said, "It's kind of awesome that she named her shop Every Woman's Fairy Godmother."

At which point I laughed. Humor washed away the remaining tension. "The name should have clued me in. I thought she was *my* fairy godmother."

"You're not exactly every woman, are you?" Her eyes darkened, and I thought—for a split second—that she might be giving me the eye. Except then she wasn't—if she ever had been. "What did she have to say about your curse?"

What had she said? I mentally shook off the attraction I shouldn't be feeling and tried to remember the specifics of the conversation. "She told me that whoever had cursed me didn't want me to remember my past."

Except they'd partially failed on that front. There was one thing I could recall from my first moment of awareness. Whoever had cursed me might have taken my memory, but they'd left me with a nasty case of guilty conscience.

But that detail I kept to myself. I didn't want to share something so personal or so ugly. Guilt was a nasty, heavy emotion.

"That's it." The clap of her hands brought me back to the present. "The more we learn about your past, the closer we'll get to solving this curse business."

"And by solving, I hope you mean breaking."

"Exactly." She followed that pronouncement up with a brilliant, knee-wobbling smile.

Good thing I was sitting down. Oh yeah, and had no physical body.

"It should be safe to delve into my past. Madeleine assured me discovery of my past wouldn't trigger any more traps."

"It *should* be safe?" Hillary leaned forward and tilted her head. She was examining me as if she could read the answer on my face.

Only one way to really know, so I gave it a shot and said, "Stephen Bradley Sherwood."

"Really?" Hillary crossed her arms, and that smile she'd blinded me with was completely gone. "That's how you make sure?"

I shrugged.

"We might need to revisit your cavalier attitude about your well-being. But for now, I want the scoop on my glasses. Did Madeleine mention them? Or why she gave me glasses that made you visible?"

I briefly considered revealing Madeleine's seeming disappointment with me. But telling an amazing woman, an intelligent, driven, kind, incredibly hot woman, that her fairy godmother's wand might have misfired, resulting in, well, me, didn't seem like a great plan.

Also, Madeleine never said exactly what the glasses were supposed to do for Hillary. So maybe her wand hadn't misfired, and the glasses had worked just fine.

And I had a perfect explanation for events. "She didn't say, but I wonder if she was trying to help you resolve Walter's housing crisis." When she arched an eyebrow, I added, "Indirectly."

"Hm. She definitely could have gone about it in a much better way. Maybe smacking Uncle Tim and Aunt Carol over the head with a magical common-sense stick or sprinkling them with some magic decency dust." She shook her head. "I'll call her and see what she says, but first, Stephen Bradley Sherwood research!"

Her enthusiasm was contagious, and I was feeling optimistic about the future for the first time in, oh, about three years.

Right up until she showed me the article she'd found.

13

HILLARY

I didn't want to show Brad the article.

I had to show him the article.

But did I? Did I really?

After more dithering, I decided that yes, I did, and showed it to him.

And I chewed my lip raw as he read it.

It was pretty clear by this point that he was either the missing twenty-six-year-old (now twenty-nine-year-old) Stephen Bradley Sherwood, or someone tied very closely to Sherwood.

The short article packed a good bit of misery into very few words...if Brad happened to be Sherwood. His girlfriend's death in a car accident (he'd been the driver), his body never found, his possible suicide, a mother left with no closure and likely suspecting the very worst outcome.

Then again, it wasn't like his mom would be suspecting the actual outcome. I could just imagine that conversation. "So sorry for the confusion, Mrs. Sherwood, but your son didn't die. He's cursed and standing in your living room right now, except he's invisible to everyone but me and my granddad."

Um, no.

Brad rubbed the back of his neck. "You might want to quit gnawing on your lip like you haven't eaten in the last three days."

I pressed my lips together. Pot, kettle. The neck rubbing was a classic tell for stress, a pretty darn obvious one, since Brad didn't have a body so he couldn't exactly have stiff muscles. I narrowed my eyes and checked for other signs of stress.

He stopped rubbing his neck. "I'm fine."

I arched an eyebrow.

"First, we don't know I'm Sherwood."

I crossed my arms.

"Fine, it's very likely I'm Sherwood. But even if I am, we'll make it right. Break the curse, tell my mom I'm alive, explain away the three years missing from my life..." He blew out a breath. "Yeah, this is gonna suck."

"Do you remember her?"

"My mom?" His eyes clouded. "No. Not my girlfriend, either, though the accident and her death might explain some uncomfortable feelings I haven't been able to shake over the last three years."

"I'll keep looking. Try to find a picture of you. You shouldn't be worrying you're this guy with this complicated past until we know for sure that you're him."

But even as I said it, I realized that Brad was going to be a guy with a complicated past *whoever* he turned out to be. Someone hated him enough to curse him, and he'd been AWOL for three years. What was more complicated than hate, magical curses, and mysterious, long-term disappearances?

This guy had over-the-airline's-weight-limit-sized baggage.

"Let's focus on the good news." He tilted his head. "Not dead, remember?"

"Oh yeah! Yes, absolutely. That is excellent news." Alive but cursed—that was the good news. I shouldn't have to remind myself of good news. "Take the wins where and when you find them" had always been in my nature.

It was all the pressure. It was getting to me and tainting my normally upbeat personality.

Gramps' evaluation was in a week, I'd only been able to completely clear my schedule for the next three days, and who knew if the person who'd cursed Brad was lurking somewhere near, waiting to zap him with *another* curse.

And if that wasn't enough pressure, what if the cursing fiend decided to zap anyone who helped Brad? Clearly the nutter had a hate-on for Brad.

Bananas. What if they decided to curse me? Or Gramps?

I couldn't even go down that path. That path led to doubt and inaction and no solution for anyone.

"You okay?" Brad asked.

"Yeah, of course."

"It's just that I asked if you had any thoughts on curse breaking and you looked like a deer caught in high-beams."

"Break the curse. Right." I flicked my hair over my shoulder, then rethought that and pulled it into a ponytail bun with a hair tie from my desk. "I need to get cracking on your past. The key to breaking the curse is there."

"Can you check in with Walter for me?" When I nodded and reached for my phone, he said, "Tell him I'm spending the night."

That made me pause, because hot guy...in my home...while I wasn't at my best. I glanced down and considered the ripped jean shorts and glittery tank I was sporting. These were my comfy clothes, and I'd slipped them on as soon as Walter dropped me off.

And I was probably modeling some gorgeous raccoon eyes. Waterproof, smudge-proof mascara was a nasty lie told by people who didn't live in extreme heat and high humidity and didn't have emotional crises.

"That's okay, right? For me to spend the night? I'll crash on the sofa if you don't have a spare room. Walter can pick me up in the morning when he brings your car by."

"He's bringing my car over?" But what was I thinking? Of course he would. My Gramps was the best. And I would give him my best, which meant delving into Brad's past and not worrying about having a hottie in the house or how sketchy I looked right now. "Hey—your clothes...is that what you were wearing when you, ah—"

"Started my life over with no memory?" Brad asked. "Yeah. Jeans and a T-shirt."

"What does 'Wild' mean?" But Brad just shook his head with a confused look, so I explained, "Your T-shirt, it says Wild on the back." The shirt was green and grey and on the front was some weird, unidentifiable animal's head with a pissed-off expression. Kind of a strange thing to get stuck wearing for three years.

"Oh, yeah, I'd forgotten about that. I'm guessing not my name, since we're eighty plus percent sure I'm Sherwood."

"Your name? Oh, like a jersey. Hang on." Before abandoning my cell on my desk, I sent Gramps a text that Brad was staying the night and we'd see him in the morning. Then I sat down and typed a few words in the search box of my browser.

It took a few seconds to find the meaning behind his shirt. As he peered over my shoulder and read the screen, I said, "You know, it's not strange that Gramps didn't recognize it. Hockey isn't such a huge sport in Texas. Not, uh, like in Minnesota."

Because Brad's T-shirt, the one he'd been wearing for three years, had been a clue to his identity that neither he nor Gramps had noticed. It looked like Brad had been a hockey fan in his former life, specifically, a fan of the Minnesota Wild.

The Minnesota Wild NHL team located in...Minnesota.

"And just because you were a fan of a sports team in Minnesota doesn't mean that you're this Stephen guy...who'd been visiting his mom in Austin from Minnesota."

Brad shook his head, but there was a smile tugging at his lips. "Knowing who I am is kinda the point, so let's just be happy we have proof."

"Pshaw. That's not proof." My fingers flew over the keys as I started to hunt the web for images of Stephen Bradley Sherwood.

I felt an odd tingle coming from my shoulder and, with a glance, saw that Brad had rested his hand there as he leaned forward to read my laptop screen.

Interesting that I could feel the contact...not that he'd felt comfortable enough with me to do that.

Brad cursed softly into my ear, and goosebumps ran up and down my arms. The good kind, which made me realize it had been a little too long since a handsome man had whispered sweet nothings in my ear.

Wait a sec.

That hadn't been an endearment.

I focused on the screen, where I found a tagged picture on a popular social media site. There was Stephen Sherwood, and he looked an awful lot like Brad.

A shirtless Brad who happened to be rocking an amazing set of abs...but that wasn't the point.

The point, I told my hormone-drenched brain, was that Stephen Bradley Sherwood and Brad were definitely one and the same.

14

HILLARY

"So do I call you Stephen or Brad?" Gramps asked before attacking his pancakes and bacon.

Brad shot Gramps a loaded look across my kitchen table.

Living with each other must have given them a good understanding of one another, because Gramps didn't hesitate—he said, "Brad it is," between bites of maple-syrup-soaked carbs.

Gramps and I shared a love of bacon and fluffy pancakes. I figured cooking for him was the least I could do after he'd delivered my car this morning. I'd even managed not to burn the bacon. Score one for Brad, because he'd supervised and prevented any kitchen disasters.

Surprise, surprise, Brad knew how to cook. And

I'm kidding, of course, because who else could have been responsible for Gramps' improved diet and sudden interest in the cooking channel? Our weekly dinners had only gotten more scrumptious as time passed, and that from a man who used to barely be able to open a can of soup.

Outside of his quiet culinary help this morning, Brad had been withdrawn ever since we discovered his true identity.

Shortly after the revelation last night, he'd excused himself and disappeared into my guest room. He'd only re-emerged when he heard me puttering around in the kitchen this morning.

I'd been about to come right out and ask if he wanted to talk about anything (say, perhaps, his real identity and what that revealed: the car crash, his mother still living and missing him, who hated him enough to curse him...), but then Gramps had shown up and the moment had been lost.

Gramps pushed his plate away after he used his last bite to sop up the remaining syrup. "You said something about a PI, peanut?"

"Oh, yes." I shot a guilty look at Brad. "After you went to bed, Mary Margaret got back in touch with a referral for a local paranormal investigator."

My reservations about this guy were large. Huge. Mountain-sized.

Brad leaned his elbows on the table. "What's that look?"

I tapped my finger on the table until I realized I was doing it and then stopped.

"Peanut?"

"Right, so this PI is highly recommended. And local." Two very interested men waited for me to spill the bad news. I groaned. "He's weird, okay? Just super, conspiracy-nut, big-brother-is-watching weird."

"Big brother *is* watching," Gramps agreed, though he didn't look particularly worried about it. "Brad explained how data is tracked and used, and I should be careful what places online I trust with my information."

Bless Brad's cautious, scam-sensitive heart. Gramps was probably less likely to become one of the many preyed-upon seniors, because Brad had taken a little time to explain the hazards in a way Gramps understood. I hadn't done that. Hadn't even thought about it till this moment.

"This guy has no social media, no website, no email, no phone number, just a PO box, and he only takes clients by referral." I could get on board with avoiding social media, but no phone number? Not even a landline? "We have to send our contact info and the job specifics to this PO box. Then we sit on our duffs and wait for him to contact us."

Brad grinned. "I think our paranormal investigator is a nostalgic soul and might be half in love with the idea of the forties detective."

Gramps nodded. "Or he's a hired killer on the side."

I choked on my coffee.

Because in all my imaginings of a what a complete kook this guy might be, that thought hadn't occurred to me.

Gramps patted my back on his way to bus his dishes. "Just because he might be an assassin, that's no reason to exclude him."

"I'm with Walter," Brad said. "And I think we should check out this PO box. Is it a USPS box? If it's not, if it's one of those little mom-and-pop shops, then we should definitely make a trip to drop the letter."

That sounded like a terrible idea, but rather than argue with the boys, I pitched my own plan. "I need to have a chat with Madeleine, and that is happening face to face, as soon as possible."

Since neither disagreed, I could only assume they were on board with my plan. Also, I might have spoken the words while exiting the kitchen to circumvent any possible disagreement.

Gramps was a tidy soul, so I knew while I changed and applied makeup, he was cleaning up the mess from breakfast, which made me feel a little bit guilty. When he cooked, he insisted I was a guest and he cleaned afterward. Sometimes I argued; frequently I had an evening appointment and left him to it.

Man, I really did need to get rid of one—or more—of my businesses. Or hire employees...which sounded exhausting.

While I primped, I came up with a plan of attack. I needed to grill my favorite shopkeeper, but I also didn't want to completely piss her off, because she had all the fabulous clothes. A girl had to have priorities, and I knew mine.

First, drag as much information about Brad and his curse—hopefully the cure—from Madeleine.

And a very, very close second: make sure I could continue shopping at Every Woman's Fairy Godmother, because she really did have the best vintage clothing in the greater Austin area.

And the next part of my plan, assuming the boys hadn't gotten over their excitement about meeting a real paranormal investigator—and I had no doubt that was why they were willing to overlook our recommended PI's foibles—I'd drop a note at a certain PO box. It couldn't be far; I recognized the zip code. And dropping my letter in person would be faster, assuming the shop would allow such a thing.

Five minutes later, I was having an argument with two adolescents.

"We're going," Brad insisted.

"You're not," I replied, and not for the first time.

"You can't leave me here without a car." Walter crossed his arms and pulled a mulish face.

"Gramps, give me a break. I know you were planning to take a rideshare back to your place." He tipped his head, as if considering fibbing, but I knew that wouldn't happen. "Look, I can drop you both at home before I head to Madeleine's."

"No," two annoyed, overprotective males replied.

"Do you really think Madeleine, my *fairy godmother*, is going to give me any problems?"

The two obnoxious men who I'd thought five minutes ago were moderately rational human beings shared a glance.

"What do you really know about her?" Brad asked.

"More than I know about you. I've known *her* five years. *You* I've known two days." Not exactly a true statement, since I'd been getting secondhand Brad stories for three years, but I thought I made my point.

"What about after?" Walter's arms were still crossed, and he was planted firmly in my exit path. No problem. I'd just go out the front door instead. "You're going to drop the note off afterward. I know you already wrote it."

I raised my eyebrows. "Is that what has you in a tizzy?"

His bushy grey eyebrows scrunched closer together as he attempted to give me a disapproving look. Gramps was terrible at disapproval.

"If that's what has you guys tied up in knots, then come with me." I raised a finger. "But you're staying in the car while I talk to Madeleine."

And that was how I ended up in the parking lot of Every Woman's Fairy Godmother giving a stern lecture more suited to children than two grown men. "Don't leave the car."

Walter frowned from the passenger seat. "It's hot."

It wasn't, not for Texas, and we were parked in the shade. I rolled down all four windows in my little orange Fiat.

"What if she's not really a fairy godmother? What if she's an evil witch?" Brad asked from the back seat.

"First, didn't she prevent you from being sent to purgatory?"

"We only have her word about that," he grumpily replied.

"And second"—I twisted around so I wasn't talking over my shoulder—"what exactly are you going to do about it?"

He scowled.

It wasn't kind to remind him of his incorporeal state, but facts were facts, and I refused to have two suddenly overprotective men meddling with a relationship I considered important to my business's success. One of my businesses' success.

"Right. So, back to the original plan: you two wait in the car, and I have a quick chat with Madeleine." I held up a hand when Walter would have continued to protest. "And my finger will be on my phone the entire time, ready to speed-dial you in case of emergency."

I got out of the car before they could delay me any further. Ridiculous, the both of them.

And yet, as I approached the front door of one of my favorite shops in Austin, for the first time ever, I felt trepidation.

15

BRAD

"Be careful, son." Walter's warning came after Hillary disappeared from sight through the front doors of Madeleine's shop.

He twisted around, then must have decided we'd have an easier time talking out of the car.

Being the upstanding guy he was, he opened the rear door for me. I could walk through walls—and car doors—but it wasn't very fun.

"I don't know what you mean." Except that was a lie. Unlike Walter, I had the basics of subterfuge down and could make a solid effort when needed. I knew exactly what he meant, or rather who he was warning me away from. Because Walter had witnessed the slow evolution of my infatuation with his granddaughter. I'd always thought he was oblivious, but I was starting to suspect he hadn't been.

He'd simply been kind not to discuss the impossibility of it.

It had only ever been a mild crush, because Hillary was out in the world, flesh and blood. I, on the other hand, was living a very small life, confined to my noncorporeal existence. And even worse than my lack of physical substance was how narrow my life had become in the absence of human interaction. Thank God for Walter, or I'd have lost my mind.

"You know." His gentle tone brought me back to the present, out of my head and into the parking lot of Every Woman's Fairy Godmother. He leaned against the shiny orange surface of Hillary's Fiat and continued in the same gentle tone, "That way lies heartache."

I rubbed my neck but didn't reply. What could I say?

"You have no body."

"We're working on that." But he was right, I didn't, and there were no guarantees.

He arched an eyebrow. "You have no memory of yourself or your previous life."

A bitter sound escaped my lips. "If you think I might be involved with someone, you're wrong. It seems my girlfriend died a year before I became this." I gestured helplessly at my insubstantial body.

"I know."

Of course he knew. Hillary must have told him, or he'd looked me up himself. I'd helped Walter become much more computer-savvy over the last few years. A simple internet search was well within his ability. And armed with my real name, he would have discovered everything that I now knew of myself.

"Then you know I'm not married or engaged. No one's waiting for me."

"That's not really the point, is it, son?"

Oh, did this man know me. He knew I carried around a terrible guilt, a guilt that for three years had held no context. But now, with the discovery of my true identity, those feelings made perfect sense.

I'd killed my girlfriend.

"Hey." His voice had sharpened. "What are you thinking? That you're not good enough or you're a bad man? It's garbage. I'm just telling you that you need to sort yourself out before you can fall for anyone—including my granddaughter."

I nodded, because he was absolutely right. I had no body, no memory of my life, and clearly some issues related to the supposed accident that had killed my girlfriend four years ago.

Small problem, though: as great as Walter's advice was, it was too late.

My little crush, the one that had been brewing through all the dinners and visits to check on her grandfather over the years, couldn't survive the reality of Hillary.

Speaking to her, watching her without reservation, seeing how she sometimes looked at me—that reality had dissolved my crush, leaving in its wake much more complex feelings.

Yeah, Walter's warning was too late.

I was already falling for Hillary.

16

HILLARY

Not a clue what I'd expected when I walked into Every Woman's Fairy Godmother.

Probably not for Madeleine to treat me as if nothing had changed.

I also hadn't expected her to tackle the topic straight on.

"Hey. I'm your fairy godmother. Have any wishes today?"

But what actually unfolded the moment I stepped through the door? Nope. Wouldn't have guessed that in a million years.

The entire place shut down like a prison on lockdown.

As I stood just inside the front door, frozen by the sound of a lock clicking into place, my astonishment only grew. After the lock turned on its own, shutters I'd swear hadn't been there when I walked into the shop closed with a resounding bang, barring the windows. And then some unseen force pulled the blind down on the glass front door.

Maybe I should have paid more attention to Walter and Brad's concerns.

"Madeleine." I should probably have removed the grump from my grumpy tone, given that she had mystical, hands-free door-locking skills, but I didn't. I crossed my arms and cocked a hip.

My patience was pretty thin, and who could blame me? I'd had a trying few days, and I hadn't slept fabulously well. Someone—a very hot guy—had invaded my dreams. And no, they were not PG.

"Don't be such a spoilsport. This is where I wow you with my mad magical skills." She wore the same welcoming smile she always did, which was comforting in the circumstances.

"Yanking my friend from the edge of oblivion already did that."

"Ah. Your friend." She bit her lip as if she was considering my response, then, after a few beats, smiled. "That's a solid argument. Either way, we needed a little privacy for this conversation. I just added a few touches for dramatic effect."

She clasped her hands in front of her and looked at me expectantly, eagerly.

Something was up. I should be looking at *her*

expectantly. I was the one who needed answers. Why was she looking at me like I held all the cards?

"So?" She bounced on her toes. I cocked my head and held silent. She prompted me again. "What do you think?"

There were so many answers to that question. So, so many. "About my grandfather's imaginary friend being real? About the fact that curses really exist? Or fairy godmothers? Or about the illegal detainment of your best client?" And that was just the tip of the iceberg.

"Oh." Madeleine deflated slightly. The bouncing stopped, in any event. "Well, that's anticlimactic."

"On what topic should I be expressing an opinion?"

She clapped her hands together like an excited child or perhaps a very enthusiastic cheerleader. And that was another reason I'd previously found her age so confusing: sometimes she seemed so mature, and others...less so.

"True love!"

Yep, today Madeleine was leaning a little more toward youthful. True love? Where did that come from? Maybe she'd just watched *The Princess Bride*. It was a pretty amazing movie.

I hated to burst her bubble, but... "There's a lot going on in my life right now. Romance isn't on my radar."

As I denied any possibility of sparkly hearts and effervescent emotions, I couldn't help thinking of Gramps' roommate. Which was ridiculous, because the man wasn't even a man. Not the touching, hugging, groping variety. Brad was a ghost. Basically.

"Are you sure about that? No romance at all?" She seemed genuinely perplexed. An opinion which she confirmed when she said, "That's not right. Not at all. I'm sure I did it correctly."

My heartbeat ticked up a notch. "Did what correctly?"

Her lips twisted, then she wrinkled her nose. "Have you worn your glasses?"

The glasses? The sunglasses. How did I forget to ask Madeleine about the sunglasses? The sparkly, couldn't-say-no, great-price, startlingly-clear-lensed, cat-eye sunglasses.

The ones that had opened my eyes to Brad.

The ones I'd completely forgotten to ask Madeleine about, because her role in yanking Brad from the very edge of purgatory had overshadowed her part in making him visible.

"You know I have. Those glasses are why I can see Brad."

She hopped and clapped her hands. "Exactly!"

I was having very mixed feelings about cheerleader Madeleine. I liked shopkeeper Madeleine so much more. Except when she was doing weird magic things to me. Then again, that was probably cheerleader Madeleine. Shopkeeper Madeleine was too busy filling my client orders to be working magic on the side.

Except they were one and the same person.

I sighed. "What did you do to the glasses?"

"The glasses were just a catalyst. The real target was you." She grinned, and a dimple appeared in her right cheek. Her grin faded when I returned her exuberance with a slight frown. "I gave you the ability to see your true love. Well, the possibility of true love. True love is tricky, because that typically happens over time. But you have to find the right person first." She smiled. "And that's what I gave you."

"You gave me the right person?"

"No, I gave you the ability to *see* the right person. 'You're welcome' wouldn't go amiss."

"I'm not thanking you for giving me something I didn't ask for."

"But you did." When I shook my head, she nodded. "Really, you did. That's my superpower as a fairy godmother: I can see what it is that you truly wish for. I can pinpoint that thing in your life that's missing and help you to find it."

"And you're telling me the something that's missing in my life is love?" She nodded, so I asked, "Love is my one true wish?"

She was still nodding, but that wasn't right. My one true wish was to sort out my grandfather's psych eval and long-term housing situation, and after that to get a handle on my businesses. Like I'd told her before, love wasn't even on my list.

"I hate to break the bad news, but I really don't think love is my one true wish."

Madeleine blinked.

At first, I thought she looked surprised, but no. I recognized the signs. Her eyes were wide, her features still, and there was the blinking.

My favorite shop owner, a magic-wielding woman of indeterminate age and a very soft and completely romantic heart, was doing her best not to cry.

I hunted in my purse for a pack of tissues and handed them to her.

"I'm fine." But as the words left her lips, a fat tear rolled down her face. She accepted the packet and pulled a tissue free. After she'd dabbed at the corners of her eyes, she said, "I'm very new at this. I'm sorry if I've cocked it up."

"You're new at being a fairy godmother?" I didn't know what to say. How did one console a magical being?

She waved a hand. "No. I've been an FG for a little while. It's the love part that's new." She flashed me a sheepish smile. "It's quite difficult, and not my cup of tea at all. Hm, perhaps I oughtn't to have said that, since you're my first subject. Drat. I likely shouldn't have said that either."

Okay, this Madeleine, the one that combined my favorite shopkeeper and the bubbly cheerleader with a dash of practical and a pinch of awkward, I found endearing.

I grinned at her. "What did you do and what was supposed to happen?"

"I'm on love duty, until... Well, for a little while. You're one of my favorite customers, *and* your heart's desire is love—romantic love—so I thought you'd be a great first client, so to speak."

Arguing about what was or wasn't my heart's desire seemed pointless, so I stuck with moving the narrative forward. Two impatient men were waiting outside, and one of them could walk through walls. "The glasses?"

"Like I said, I gave them a little FG kick"—she made a motion that looked more like sprinkling than tweaking, which then made me wonder if fairy godmother dust was a thing—"and *voila*, you can see your one true love. Well, the most likely possibility for true love."

A half-muffled snort escaped. Yes, she was in a delicate state, but please—my most likely possibility for true love was a guy who was practically a ghost?

Either Madeleine's newbie skills had failed or the universe was laughing at me.

She wrinkled her nose, looking simultaneously cute, dismayed, and disappointed. "He wasn't supposed to be cursed." Her face settled into a more passive expression, but she still looked a bit worried. "I'm not terribly old for an FG, and it was perhaps a tad ambitious for me to accept this particular post, but I didn't really have much choice, and—well, something might have gone slightly awry, but the underlying magic is sound. Stephen—"

"Brad. He hasn't gotten his memory back yet. He prefers Brad."

She smiled. It was a small smile, but a definite improvement. "The underlying magic is sound, I promise. I'm quite good with the basics. Brad could be your true love, don't you think?" She cleared her throat. "If he was corporeal, naturally."

Was corporeal Brad a guy I'd date? If I was honest with myself—and if I was actually dating, which I wasn't at the moment—then yes.

Yes times ten might be more accurate.

Incredibly good-looking, that Clark Kent thing that had him appearing in my X-rated dreams, the washboard abs I now knew were under his Wild T-shirt (those abs had a starring role in my dreams), and that didn't even touch on what an amazing man he was.

The guy had pulled my grandfather from a robe-wearing, hygiene-optional, canned-food-dependent depressive slump back into the land of the living. And he'd done that all while lacking an ability to interact with the physical world.

Brad was kind of a badass.

A sweet, kind, adorable (okay, real talk, incredibly hot) badass.

He was also cursed by some unknown person to live a life with no physical form and had no memory of his previous life.

"I think your question is moot, because there are hurdles." I pressed my lips together. "Significant hurdles."

My cautious reply should not have elicited the brilliant, practically incandescent, smile Madeleine bestowed on me. "Let's chat about those hurdles."

17

HILLARY

The letter I'd penned earlier to our finicky PI was short.

He seemed the kind who might be attracted to intrigue, and maybe (I hoped) he'd read some mystery into a message that contained few facts and only alluded to the problem.

I'd also promised prompt cash payment for results, because money tended to be a popular motivator. Between the mystery and the cash, I was hopeful he'd take an interest.

But either way, I didn't expect a quick reply. It was likely going to be a few days, at best, before our PI got the letter. Maybe faster if the post shop would drop the letter directly in his box—that was probably against all kinds of federal regulations, so I wasn't holding my breath—and slower if the guy didn't check his box regularly.

I should have a better idea shortly, because we were en route to the post shop now.

"Are you really not going to tell us what Madeleine had to say?" Brad asked from the passenger seat.

I hadn't a clue how Walter had ended up in the back and Brad in the front, but since my shotgun passenger wasn't visible to the world at large, I had to look like a loon talking to thin air and chauffeuring around an old guy in the back of my tiny Fiat.

"Are you really going to make me have a conversation with an invisible person while I drive in Austin traffic?"

"No one notices what other people are doing in their cars, peanut." I glanced at Gramps in my rearview mirror and found him sprawled as best he could across my back seat. He grinned at me. "There's more room back here than I thought there'd be."

Since he'd given me grief when I bought the car, I took that as belated approval of my darling Sophia. Yes, I'd named my car. Didn't everyone?

"Madeleine?" Brad prompted.

"Right. Madeleine." Except I didn't want to talk about Madeleine.

Or what Madeleine had to say about me.

And Brad.

Together.

I could go with something like "So, Brad, Madeleine might claim to be a fairy godmother, but she's really more of love doctor. An inept, magic-wielding love doctor. And according to her, you're my huckleberry."

Or I could not say that. For so many reasons.

"It's bad news, isn't it?" The movement of Brad's knee bouncing up and down caught my eye.

Was it bad news? Surprising, maybe. I hadn't spent my few off hours planning my future wedding (though I'd go with low-key, close friends and family only) or imagining my wedding gown (ivory, not white; white would wash me out) or have a ring picked out (I liked sapphires, not diamonds). And I hadn't thought about doing deliciously dirty things with a certain Clark Kent lookalike.

Okay, that last part was an outright lie, because I had thought about a shirtless (maybe pantsless) Brad. Naked Brad was yummy. Who would blame me? Especially subconscious me, the me who was driving the bus during my dreams.

And, clearly, I'd given more thought to coupling up than I'd realized, since I already had my nonexistent fiancé out buying me a sapphire and was walking down the aisle in an ivory gown with a small group watching.

Wow. Maybe romance was higher on my priority list than I realized? Or it wasn't but should be?

"Peanut, you need to spill, before Brad has a coronary—if that's possible when you don't have a body."

"You can tell me. The curse isn't breakable, is it?" Brad's knee was still bouncing at a disturbingly fast rate.

Bananas. My crisis was not *the crisis*. I was a selfish twit.

I pulled into the strip mall parking lot where the post shop was located and parked. Then I turned all of my attention to Brad. One hundred percent of my focus was on him and his problem—not me and my romantic woes.

Ninety-eight percent.

Eighty-something percent.

Brad's nervous knee did a jig.

Focus, Hillary.

So I did, and I shared what I'd learned in the last few minutes of my conversation with Madeleine, which wasn't much. "I asked her about breaking your curse, and while she didn't know exactly how to do that, she said that every curse has an out clause. Some have more than one. 'No curse is unbreakable,' and that's a direct quote. She seemed pretty hopeful."

Not that I was going to explain *why* she'd been hopeful. In order for Brad and me to pair up and for Madeleine to check the box for her first love doctor duty accomplished, Brad had to be corporeal. So of course she was hopeful.

"How do we find my out clause?" Brad asked, and finally, his knee stopped its frantic bounce.

"We find who cursed you. Madeleine said curses take a lot of powerful emotion to create"—hate was the actual word she'd used, but I couldn't say that. Who could hate Brad? He was basically the nicest guy ever—"and that delving into the details behind the emotion would reveal the way to break the curse."

"That's incredibly vague." Brad's knee agreed with him, because it started up its nervous dance again.

Walter leaned between the two front seats. "We need more information about Brad's past, and we're dinking around in the car rather than chasing up an avenue of investigation."

Since when did my grandfather say "dinking around"? But he had a point. "Let's do this."

I had my doubts about this PI—what did a paranormal investigator even do?—but he came highly recommended. And we were here.

And he could only help, right? He couldn't make the situation worse...unless *he* sent Brad to purgatory.

"What's with the groaning, peanut?"

I leaned against Gramps as he paused in front of the post shop's door. "Just thinking unpleasant thoughts about purgatory."

He squeezed my shoulder reassuringly before opening the door.

"Let's not talk about that. I'm trying to stay positive." Brad waited for me to precede him through the door then followed closely on my heels before Gramps stepped through.

A positive attitude was a good start. It was better than anxious and on edge, which was what he'd been in the car, in large part due to my mini freak-out about Madeleine's attempts to fulfill my secret (even to me) deepest wish.

Although, honestly, I'd be freaking out if I was Brad. I'd probably have freaked out for three years, because as much as I loved my grandfather, I couldn't imagine him as my only source of companionship for years at a time.

And then there was purgatory.

I shuddered. "You're right. That P-word can stay where it belongs: far away from you."

The clerk, a small, wiry, unshaven man behind the counter, raised his eyebrows at my comment, which out of context might seem weird. And maybe sexual? Oops.

"Hi." I offered him a bright smile. A little charm made everything easier. I was a child of the South and firmly believed that to be true. Also, I was about to ask this guy for a favor, and I really didn't want him thinking I was a weirdo.

His returning smile was polite, but only just. "How can I help you?"

"I need to deliver a letter to a post box here. It's an emergency, so I was hoping you could drop it directly into the box."

His smile disappeared. "You have an emergency letter?"

Hm. That did sound weird. I hadn't really contemplated my backstory. I glanced at Gramps (no help there, since he was Mr. Truth and Honesty) then at Brad (who shrugged). Great.

When no response to his question was forthcoming, the clerk said, "That's highly irregular, and I'm not sure it's legal. I'd have to check." But then his annoyed expression eased slightly, and he asked, "Which box?"

"Seventy-four," Gramps chimed in, reading the number from the envelope clenched in my fingers.

Once again, the clerk's demeanor changed. I couldn't read his expression, but he no longer looked like he'd chugged sour milk straight from the carton. "Ah, that's fine. I can take it."

Right. Like that wasn't weird.

I must have been pretty transparent, because with supremely fake nonchalance, he said, "I'll deliver it now."

"Any chance this guy is an agent for the investigator?" Brad asked.

An agent? Nope. For the clerk's benefit and also in reply to Brad, I said, "I don't think so."

The clerk looked confused. "Do you want me to deliver it or not?"

"No," Gramps replied. He'd picked up on the same thing I had.

Together, we both turned to the exit.

"Uh, guys?" Brad, the one person in the room with real skin in the game, didn't see what Gramps and I did. Stress could do that, make the obvious invisible. I winked at him. And yes, it felt as goofy as it sounds, but he got the message and relaxed a bit.

"Wait," the clerk called as we reached the door. "You have a, ah, a *special* problem?"

I stopped and gave the clerk a second, more thorough look.

That confirmed it. This was the guy.

Bananas.

Nope, worse. Banana nut bread, heavy on the nuts. Mr. Unkempt Beard Guy didn't instill high levels of confidence in his paranormal investigative skills. And breaking a curse? Yeah...no. I didn't see this guy out fighting the magical fight and kicking curse butt.

Then again, looks could be deceiving, and we could use some professional help.

"Right" I peered at his name tag—"Smitty. How do you feel about breaking curses?"

His eyes lit up, and he stood taller. Rubbing his hands together, he said, "Now we're talking."

Yep. We sure were. We were talking to the mail clerk with a big-brother complex about breaking a curse of unknown origin on a guy he couldn't see.

Fun times.

But then I caught the hopeful look on Brad's face, and I gave Smitty my most genuine smile. "We would appreciate your help."

18

HILLARY

Turned out my first impression of Smitty was slightly askew.

Smitty the mail clerk was actually Archibald Schmidt, the post shop's owner. He claimed "Smitty" made him seem more approachable, and I wasn't going to disabuse him of the notion. He'd been in the paranormal investigating business for five years. He liked using the post box, because it was convenient for him and allowed him to screen the crazies out without having to engage with them firsthand.

We were only the second prospective client to show up at the post shop. Which meant that Smitty wasn't the loon in this scenario. Yes, that would be me. Or Gramps and I, though Gramps had been letting me run the investigative show thus far, so it was hard to put any of the crazy on him.

Smitty wasn't a conspiracy nut. He wasn't into intrigue, he wasn't an assassin on the side, and he wasn't a wannabe secret agent. No, he was just a guy with a little bit of common sense trying to minimize the nut jobs he came into contact with, because his job attracted them.

I wasn't a nut job, though. I was completely sane. Just call me the not-crazy woman sharing her grandfather's delusion.

But Smitty was really nice about us showing up, and we managed to get a little info from him before a regular (not paranormal) client appeared.

Brad, Gramps, and I learned that over the past five years, Smitty had encountered some creepy, otherworldly beings, including ghosts (which Brad clearly wasn't, since the shop's spectral sensors hadn't gone off) and witches (who Smitty believed might be responsible for Brad's current dilemma).

That was as far as we made it (just ghosts and witches) before a lady with an armful of wedding invitations walked into the store.

We left not knowing if Smitty had any specialized knowledge about breaking Brad's curse or if he had decent regular PI skills and could help us dig into Brad's history.

On the plus side, Smitty had displayed a child-like giddiness at the opportunity to help us. If he could help, he would; that much was clear. He'd even waived our offer of renumeration.

"Expenses only," he'd replied.

But the flip side of Smitty's enthusiasm was the concern that he hadn't experienced a huge amount of paranormal action in his five years as investigator. He *wanted* to help, but *could* he?

As Gramps, Brad, and I waited the thirty minutes Smitty said he needed to get backup at the store, I wasn't so sure.

To pass the time, Gramps chatted about his new audiobook app (which he adored), his new neighbor (who he loved less due to the man's decision to raze the home he'd just purchased rather than renovate it), and his recent decision to adopt a dog (which I couldn't be happier about).

I listened, but contributed little, because reasons.

Okay, I might have been distracted. Ever since my meeting with Madeleine, I had sex on the brain. Actually, I'd always had sex on the brain. Now I had sex and *love* on the brain.

Gramps kept the conversation flowing. I mostly dithered over love, work, and romance and what it all meant for me and my current life. Brad watched us both, participating when appropriate, but staying mostly quiet.

When Smitty arrived, we breathed a collective sigh of relief.

Then he set his coffee down on the edge of the table, barely catching it before it tipped over.

And *then* he almost sat on top of Brad.

Not a particularly promising beginning.

We'd chosen a four-top table outside, and it was a little on the warm side since there was no shade, so no one was around to see our shenanigans or overhear our conversation. Thank goodness, because Smitty's response was comically overblown. He even apologized to Brad.

"Maybe he's like an absent-minded professor," Brad said. "He lives in his head, so he's awkward."

"Hm." I was reserving judgment. At least until I heard more about witches and curses. If he could give us a leg up on breaking Brad's curse, I'd hug him. If not? Then we'd part ways.

"I'm with Brad," Gramps said. He tended to give people the benefit of the doubt, so that wasn't a surprise. Rubbing his hands together, he added, "And I want to hear about ghosts and witches."

Smitty's eyes widened with intense curiosity as he took in the three of us, or at least Gramps, me, and Brad's chair.

An unpleasant thought surfaced, and it had everything to do with psychiatrists, competency hearings, and my dwindling reliability as a witness in any forthcoming proceedings.

"Do you offer your clients an assurance of confidentiality, Smitty?" I leaned so I was more directly in his line of sight. He couldn't seem to take his eyes off Brad (or Brad's chair).

Smitty frowned then seemed to gather himself. "Absolutely. I guarantee discretion." He lowered his voice. "How long has Brad been with you?"

"Three years," Gramps replied.

"But I've only been able to see him for a few days."

Smitty looked between us with no effort to hide his curiosity. "That must have been awkward."

"I assumed Brad was his imaginary friend."

"And I never doubted he was real." Gramps shrugged. "Not after the first few months."

"Interesting." Smitty looked at the two of us for a few more seconds then shook his head. "How did you come to the conclusion that Brad's cursed and not a ghost? Not that I'm arguing. I have the shop wired for ghosts, and he didn't set off any alarms."

Which was the point at which I had to fess up about my fairy godmother.

I'd confessed to a lot of embarrassing events in my life—chemically straightening my hair (I was young), throwing up in my Aunt Carol's bathroom sink (I was legit sick, not a hangover in sight, not that she believed me), teal mascara (it was just the once, I swear), a pixie cut (so pretty on others; not on me)—but telling a grown man, however accepting of the paranormal he might be, that I'd had an encounter with my fairy godmother? That might top my embarrassing confessions list.

Nothing to it but to do it.

So I told him about Madeleine and how she'd yanked Brad away from the very edge of purgatory, and then how I'd confronted her and she'd told me Brad was cursed and she was my FG. I skipped over the love and romance bits, because I had my limits, but did mention the glasses.

Telling a stranger that Brad was potentially the love of my life when I didn't know how I felt about that—no. Telling a stranger that same thing when the object of my maybe-love sat less than a foot away—no, no, no, and no.

"This lady, Madeleine, she grants your wishes?" Smitty seemed skeptical, and who could blame the guy? We were talking about *a fairy godmother*. The movies and cartoons hadn't done Madeleine and her kind any huge favors.

"No. I didn't wish for anything." That wasn't a fib. I had never articulated my supposed deepest wish for true love. Heck, I wasn't even one hundred percent sold that love was one of my top three wishes. Sure, everyone wanted to fall in love, to find that special someone who was their other half, the person they looked forward to seeing at the end of a long day, the person they called in the middle of particularly difficult day, the person—

Oh. My. God.

First the wedding gown and engagement ring, and now this. Madeleine was right. Buried deep, deep down, I'd been longing for a special someone... someone to love.

Ack.

"Are you okay?" Brad asked.

"Yeah. Of course. I'm fine."

"Peanut, you checked out of the conversation for a bit."

"Oh." I patted Gramps' hand. "I'm good. I'm sorry, Smitty, what were you saying?"

"Just expressing some reservations about someone who called themselves a fairy godmother. She's not a witch?"

"Hold on. She mentioned witches. Something about FGs being the cooler cousin of witches, except with better magic. Oh! And nicer. Or something like that."

"She did help you see Brad, so she obviously has magic. She couldn't break the curse herself?"

Brad explained how Madeleine had rescued him from purgatory and altered the curse to keep him safe from future trips, and Gramps repeated everything for Smitty.

"She's got magic, strong magic, but not enough to break the curse. Interesting." Smitty pulled out a notepad and pen. "My first fairy godmother. All right. Let's set aside this issue for a moment. How is it Walter can see Brad?" Smitty asked. Seeing our confused faces, he added, "Brad's curse is to be unseen. To live amongst people, but not with them. To be in the world but not of it. It's a pretty terrible as far as curses go."

No one was arguing that. Brad himself had said that he wasn't sure his sanity would have survived the last three years without Walter for company.

Smitty tapped his forefinger on the table near me. "You can see Brad because your fairy godmother—"

"FG." I winced, because every time he said "fairy godmother" in that slightly bemused tone, I envisioned something, someone, very unlike Madeleine. "That's how she refers to herself."

"Fine. Your FG bent Brad's curse enough for you to see him. What about Walter? How can Walter see him?"

Walter, Brad, and I exchanged glances, and each of us was as stumped as the other. Finally, Walter replied, "Maybe I have an FG."

Smitty gave Gramps a look, the kind filled with

skepticism, but not overtly so. The sort of look that masqueraded as polite interest, but really meant: you're a crazy person.

"What? Hillary has one. Why can't I?" Gramps looked at me. "You said something before, about how an FG senses what you need."

I had said that. I hadn't explained what Madeleine had sensed in me, but I'd mentioned the general concept.

Gramps tipped his head in my direction. "She can tell you that three years ago I needed a friend. Someone outside of my family, someone who hadn't known Ingrid, my late wife. And then Brad showed up."

Huh. Sounded like FG intervention to me, if Madeleine's whole deepest desire schtick was to be believed. And like me, Gramps probably wouldn't have articulated a new BFF as his greatest wish at the time, but that was what he'd needed. Hindsight being twenty-twenty, it was sparklingly clear that he'd needed Brad to help him turn a difficult corner in his life.

"Let's shelve that for now." Smitty scrubbed his hand across his beard. "What did your FG have to say about breaking Brad's curse? I assume you asked."

"Yes!" Eventually. After Madeleine and I had discussed her role in my love life. "She said every curse has an out clause and that if we found the person who cursed Brad and figured out why he was cursed, that should give us insight into how to break the curse."

"An out clause." Smitty nodded. "Interesting. Different language, but similar concept to what I've heard before."

"Have you seen a curse broken before?" Brad leaned closer, forgetting that Smitty couldn't see or hear him.

Gramps repeated the question, and Brad sat back with his arms crossed as he waited to hear the answer.

Three years of cursed living, three years with no body...so how did he stay in such amazing shape?

Because Brad did. He *so* did. His biceps bulged under the short sleeves of his Wild T-shirt. I couldn't help but notice. When the guy was basically flashing arm porn, how could I not?

"Hillary? You okay?" Brad uncrossed his arms and leaned toward me.

"Absolutely." I was definitely not okay. I kept missing chunks of the conversation, and this stuff was important. Madeleine had messed with my head, and I needed my head one hundred percent un-messed with right now.

"Like I was saying." Smitty rubbed his hands together. "There are two ways to break a curse. This doesn't seem like the religious variety, so that just leaves the loophole. Your FG calls it an out clause. All magic has a cure or a loophole. Except for death. I think that's pretty permanent."

And he wasn't kidding. He *thought* that was pretty permanent, but he wasn't sure. Way to freak me out, Smitty. "But Brad's not dead, so that's moot."

Smitty glanced at Brad's empty chair. "Yeah, I guess."

Gramps smacked the table. "He had an aura. We forgot all about that. The psychic nun saw Brad's aura."

Instead of looking at Gramps like he was a crazy person, Smitty smiled, revealing a surprisingly white, even set of teeth. "Mary Margaret? She's the best. If she read his aura and said he's alive, then he's alive."

Interesting. Smitty knew of Mary Margaret, but she hadn't known about him. She'd gotten his info from a third party. Maybe Mary Margaret was a bigger deal in the paranormal world than I'd realized. Not that it mattered. She was good people, and that was enough for me.

"The loophole?" Brad asked.

"Right, so how do we find the loophole?" Gramps asked, without translating Brad. "Hillary's FG said to find out more about Brad's background. Can you help us with that?"

"We have a name, a news article, and the name of his mother, but that's all," I added.

Brad tensed at the mention of his mother. "You can't approach my mother. That's, ah, that's not..." He looked confused and pretty darn upset for a guy who couldn't even remember the woman he was trying to protect.

"Hey." Gramps twisted around to face Brad. "We won't do that. That would be unkind, and we wouldn't do that."

Since I hated absolutes, I said, "We won't approach her without talking to you first." Because if it came to saving Brad at the expense of temporarily upsetting his mother, so be it. I'd bet my dog-walking business that she'd just be glad to have her son back.

"I thought he didn't have any memory?" Smitty asked.

"He doesn't," Gramps said. "But he gets these strong emotional responses to certain things."

"I do?" Brad asked as I said, "He does?"

"Driving without wearing a seatbelt." Gramps pointed a finger at me. "Don't start. You know I'm safe. It was one time, and I hadn't left the driveway. Brad, remember, there was that dog on that commercial."

Gramps' vague description elicited a nod from Brad, and his cheeks pinked. He cleared his throat.

"Yeah, I forgot about that. There was also that one song they play on that other commercial."

Gramps repeated Brad's comment for Smitty.

"Interesting," Smitty replied. "It looks like the curse buried his memory rather than erasing it. That's good news. The person who placed the curse didn't have enough juice to eradicate his past life."

"Good. We need all the help we can get. I've got a psychiatric evaluation late this week." Gramps still looked thoroughly unruffled by the prospect. If only I had his faith in my aunt and uncle's intentions.

"Ah," Smitty said. "Go ahead and give me Brad's and his mother's names and some details from the article you found."

I blinked in confusion while Gramps filled him in. Gramps told him about his upcoming meeting with a psychiatrist, and he'd said, "Ah"?

Once Gramps had recapped the article, Smitty tapped his pen against the paper for a few seconds then said, "The girlfriend's family, have you had any contact with them?"

Oh. Oooh. Someone had died. Someone who was likely loved by her family. A family who might hold Brad responsible.

Gramps' thoughts must have been running parallel to my own, because he said, "We need to find out more about the accident."

"I'm such an idiot." I rubbed my temples,

avoiding Brad's gaze. "The article even said that Brad disappeared on the first anniversary of his girlfriend's death."

"Hey." I felt the warm tingle of Brad's almost-touch on my shoulder. "We weren't even sure I was Sherwood until late yesterday, and then there were other details to sort out—like figuring out why I had an aura."

Smitty cleared his throat. "Next thing on the agenda, find the family of the girl. And when we do, I'll bet you they're witches."

Angry almost-in-laws who were witches. And we didn't know what had happened over four years ago in that car crash.

I believed the name of the emotion I was currently feeling was called dread.

19

HILLARY

Before we parted ways with Smitty, Gramps had asked him if he could get the accident report, and while Smitty didn't make any promises, he agreed to try.

He also said he'd be having a look at Brad's girlfriend's family...cautiously.

"Anyone else disappointed?" I asked my passengers. "First, there's Madeleine with her 'every curse can be broken' and 'investigate Brad's past.' Generic and not helpful. Then we get Smitty with his 'loophole' and 'the witches did it.' How does that help us?"

"Calm down and pay attention to the road." Gramps was once again in the front seat.

Brad was in the back, probably digesting the complete lack of progress we'd been making. His fingers brushed against my arm. "What happened to staying positive?"

Maybe he wasn't as disappointed by our outing as I was.

His touch was oddly reassuring, given there was no actual contact. The only reason I knew he was touching me was the oddly warm tingles I felt—and I didn't want him to stop. He could keep on touching me, and that would be just fine.

The sad thing? I didn't even mean that in the pervy sense.

Gramps' phone pinged, and Brad's hand fell away from my arm.

Brad and I waited anxiously while Gramps checked his email. He'd passed along his address to Smitty, commenting that anything from our paranormal expert might get lost amongst the tsunami of email I received.

After a few seconds, the entirety of which I kept my attention on the road, Gramps said, "Grace Galloway."

A quickly inhaled breath from the back seat told me that Brad recognized the name.

Gramps skimmed his email, then said, "That's the name of the woman who died, but that's all Smitty has so far. He's certainly quick."

Brad didn't comment, and Gramps—who knew Brad far better than me—didn't push him.

I dropped Gramps at home, and after a brief discussion, we all decided Brad would come home with me. I was about to do some digging, and he wanted to be present for it.

The ride home was rough. It probably didn't help that I pushed. I couldn't help it; I felt protective of Brad. He was just such a nice guy. A nice guy I had a major crush on. Maybe more than a crush.

Which made me think of Madeleine and her "possibility of true love" schtick. If she was to be believed, Brad was my possibility of true love. Maybe I got more than one of those in a lifetime?

Or maybe I didn't, which was just too depressing, considering my possible one and only true love was currently doomed to a life with no physical contact.

That was a mood killer, assuming the mood hadn't already been murdered with a hatchet and disarticulated.

Wow. I didn't do well with the thought of thwarted love. Not that I was in love with a guy I'd met two days ago. Because that would be ridiculous.

After the silence became too great, I said, "The article made it sound like an accident."

Not a peep from the back seat.

"You know the papers always mention if drugs or alcohol are involved in an auto accident."

A noncommittal grunt was his reply.

"You're not guilty just because you were there."

"I wasn't just there. I was driving." An interesting response, because I couldn't recall if the article had definitively identified Brad as the driver.

So I asked, "Is that your memory talking?"

"Not a memory so much as a certainty. I just *know* that I was, but I don't remember the accident. Or Gigi. Or actually driving."

"Gigi?" The wheels in my head were spinning. Gigi. Grace Galloway, initials G.G. No way had Brad pulled that nickname from anywhere but his memory.

A lengthy pause followed. Eventually, Brad said, "Grace."

That was it, just Grace. No explanation for the nickname he'd pulled from memories that should be deeply buried.

"Maybe Smitty will find out something about Grace's family. They're looking like the most likely source of your curse."

But really, who was a likely candidate when it came to magical grudges and wicked curses? Those people—if they were people—lived in a different universe than the one I inhabited on a daily basis. Did witches—if we truly were dealing with witches—have the same motivations as non-magical people?

Logic said it had to be one of Grace's family who was responsible, or a friend, because Brad had been cursed on the anniversary of Grace's death. And since magic was out of my realm of comprehension, I'd just have to stick with logic.

"I know you don't remember her, but does the idea of Grace as a witch ring any bells, maybe jog loose anything in your memory?"

"No, that doesn't resonate."

Which left me with friends and family. "How about a disapproving father? An older brother who wanted to kick your butt? A mom who thought her daughter could do better?"

Brad groaned. "I just don't know."

"Right. Sorry." Pushing wasn't helping, so I left him to his broody thoughts in the back of my Fiat. We'd be home in just a few minutes anyway.

20

BRAD

Two hours of looking over Hillary's shoulder and I felt like punching a wall. Except I was physically incapable of punching anything, a wall included, and I wasn't the kind of guy who derived satisfaction from smashing things.

Looked like I was in a standoff. With myself.

"You look like you need a break." Hillary peered up at me from her desk chair. "Seriously. I'm the one typing and getting the sore mouse-clicking finger, but you're the one looking wiped."

"It's frustrating watching you dig through all of these articles without being able to help."

She chewed on her lower lip, which had me staring. I'd love to brush my thumb across it, to stop her from marring the plump flesh of her lip and also to simply be able to touch her in such an intimate way.

She stopped suddenly. "I suspect it's even more frustrating to find basically nothing about Grace Galloway or her family online."

I ran a hand through my hair. "Yeah, that too. I don't understand with all the details we have why we can't find more about the accident or about her and her family."

"Maybe it's magic?" She flashed me a crooked smile.

"Or maybe she was social media shy."

"That's an awfully practical viewpoint, but it doesn't explain the lack of news stories."

No, it wouldn't. Maybe no one had cared—but that felt wrong, and it triggered a rush of guilt.

That terrible, clinging, cloying, never-ending guilt. I felt responsible for Grace's death in my bones or my gut or my ectoplasm. Whatever part of me that remained attached to this world, I felt it there. Sometimes the weight of it was so strong that I had a physical reaction.

Like now.

My stomach felt sour. A real trick when I couldn't eat.

These feelings had to mean something. Why would I be experiencing them if I were innocent? And I *had* been driving—that much I knew. And the woman who'd died, she must have been someone I loved.

And that added more turmoil to the mix; anger this time. I'd loved a woman, someone who no longer walked this earth, and yet I held not one single memory of her in my head.

Not to mention the absence of any recollection of my family. Not the mother the newspaper article mentioned. Not any siblings, if I had them. And not my father, who was strangely absent from any reporting Hillary and I had seen.

Hillary's phone chirped.

She picked it up absent-mindedly, but after a glance, her attention sharpened. "This is from Gramps. He's forwarding a link he got from Smitty." She gave me an approving look. "Good job with the texting lessons. I didn't know he knew how to do that."

"What is it?"

"It's a website." She tapped the screen, then turned to her computer and started typing.

After a few seconds, she tipped her laptop screen back so I could better see the web page.

It was almost like someone had kneed me in the groin. The pain was sudden and low in my stomach, and I couldn't quite catch my breath. I bent over with my hands on my knees and struggled to catch my breath.

Panic followed quickly on the heels of the pain. Had Madeleine failed in her attempt to keep me in the land of the living? Was I headed to purgatory?

But the pain receded, and a warm, tingling sensation ran up and down my back. I cocked my head to find Hillary rubbing my back.

Rubbing my back...and I could feel it. Not that it felt like someone touching me. Human contact may not exist in my three years of memory, but I had an understanding of it.

When I finally stood up, Hillary asked, "Are you okay?" Then she scanned my face. "It's her?"

I couldn't answer. I told myself I hadn't caught my breath, but I didn't even nod.

The computer screen sucked me in, and I found myself staring.

The site looked like a virtual memorial. It was hard to say for sure, because there was no text on the page, just pictures of the same girl over and over again. But it *felt* like a memorial. The young woman in the pictures was maybe just out of college, twenty-two or twenty-three, pretty, dark-haired, and petite.

And so familiar.

"You're definitely okay?" When I nodded, and after giving me a thorough head-to-toe examination, Hillary scrolled to the bottom of the page. "If this is Grace Galloway, Smitty is really good, because I don't see her name anywhere."

"It's her."

Hillary's phone pinged again. She glanced at it and said, "A text from Gramps telling me to check my email."

She opened her email, and I read it over her shoulder. It looked like Smitty hadn't found the kind of news trail he'd expected with a tragic death, but he *did* find a friend of Grace's who was willing to talk about Grace and the accident.

"He's cleverer than he looks." Hillary wrinkled her nose. "That sounded unkind."

"No, you're right. There's a bumbling, incompetent air about him, but he's given us some helpful tips in very short order."

"Oh, wow." She'd continued to read, as had I, and must have gotten to the bottom. "Adele Galloway, Grace's mom, is her only close surviving family member."

"And the accident site is local, just outside of Austin."

Hillary spun her chair around and squinted. Her piercing look made me a little uncomfortable. "The friend Smitty interviewed says the site is marked."

"Yeah, I read that." The back of my neck felt pinched.

Whoever had cursed me was diabolical. None of the advantages of a body, but I could still ache, feel queasy, and experience pain. The desire to kick his

—or more likely her, since Adele Galloway was looking like our best candidate—butt was pretty damn strong. Except I wasn't a violent guy.

The fact that I'd reminded myself twice in less than an hour that I didn't normally like to hit people or things was probably an excellent indicator of my current state of mind.

Also, it was completely possible that pre-memory-loss Brad (a.k.a. Stephen Sherwood) was a bad-tempered guy with anger and violence issues. Probably not, because I didn't *feel* like that kind of guy. But I couldn't know for sure.

"So?" Hillary said.

Her meaning was clear: visit the crash site or not? But there was only one answer. "Let's go."

"And Gramps?"

I was shaking my head before I'd formulated a response. *Danger, danger* flashed in my head, with red lights and warning bells. Maybe the location of a witch's death was especially important. Maybe it was a trap and my cursed sixth sense was stepping up to warn me.

And if it wasn't safe for Walter, then... "Actually, maybe it's best you don't come with me."

Hands on her hips, she said, "Uh-huh. And how exactly are you going to get there. The bus?"

"Yeah, and walk."

She grabbed her keys and headed for the door.

"You go your way. I'll go mine. We'll see who gets there faster." Then she jingled the keys in the air over her shoulder.

A few curse words flitted through my head, but I refrained from articulating them. She was trying to help, and by now it was pretty darn clear that she was doing it for me, not just because solving my problem helped solve Walter's.

I rode shotgun. What else was I going to do? But I spent the first several minutes in silence, kind of pissed off. I felt powerless without a body—invisible and powerless. Having Hillary completely ignore my concern for her safety didn't help one iota.

It didn't matter that Hillary was basically unstoppable, by a ghostly presence, a flesh-and-blood man, or anyone else. If I had locked her in the pantry, she still would have found a way out and followed me.

Which was pretty amazing.

She was amazing.

Also, I would never lock anyone in a pantry, especially not Hillary.

"Why are you smiling? Oh! Did you remember something?" She anxiously tapped her fingers on the steering wheel.

"No. I like your nail polish. The way it makes your nails sparkle is really you."

She grinned broadly. "Thanks. I love this color. Gramps disapproves. He thinks anything but pink is too modern. Gray-blue with shimmery sparkles isn't up to his sartorial standards."

A harsh laugh escaped. It came out rough and rusty, probably because I didn't laugh all that much these days. I got by just fine on a day-to-day basis, but a sense of fun and joy eluded me. Being cursed would do that.

"Your grandfather lived in a terry cloth robe from the seventies for who knows how long before I moved in. I'm pretty sure he's not allowed to comment on anyone else's sense of fashion."

"He would never. He's too nice. Oh my gosh." She snickered. "You remember the pleated pants?"

Pleated jeans, pleated corduroys, pleated khakis. Not to say that pleats were never good, but I could safely say they were never good on Walter.

"I do. I made sure those were burned." Not literally, obviously. Walter was a frugal soul and couldn't stand to see good clothing go to waste. I convinced him there was a needy guy out there who would appreciate all those pleats. I was sure that guy existed, and I was sure Walter's pants looked much better on him.

"Oh my gosh. I'm a terrible person. He should wear whatever he likes." She paused with a conflicted look on her face, so I waited for the professional shopper in her to rise to the surface.

She let out a breath. "Except pleats. He really shouldn't wear pleats."

We drove without speaking for several minutes. It was nice, the shared quiet with no awkward tension. Walter and I shared silence well, but this was different.

Hillary's gaze slid sideways and lingered on me for a few heartbeats. "It's not much further."

I nodded, but then she looked at me again, so I asked, "Something on your mind?"

"Have you considered that seeing the crash site might bring your memory back?"

No. It hadn't even crossed my mind. If I had a body, I'd be sweating right about now. In the calmest tone I could manage, I said, "That would solve a lot of problems."

She made a noncommittal noise.

If our understanding (my understanding) of the crash thus far was correct, I'd been driving. I'd very likely seen a woman die, and that woman had been someone I'd loved. Or at least someone I'd cared enough about to date.

That I might regain those memories filled me with both terror and hope.

"There's no real reason to think that...is there?" I wiped my palms on my jeans, even though I knew I wasn't actually sweating.

"I don't know. With some context, you remembered Gigi."

I wasn't sure if she meant the nickname or the woman, but either way, she wasn't wrong. There was something...something just on the edge of my awareness, but the harder I tried to grab it, the more it slipped away.

I turned to watch the passing landscape in the hopes it might trigger some scrap of a memory.

And I thought about Grace. Gigi.

The names were at odds with one another. Grace was a simple, elegant, old-fashioned name. Gigi much less so. The woman on the site had looked like a Gigi. Vibrant, cheerful, fun. That woman wasn't a Grace. She was a Gigi.

Which was absolutely ridiculous. What did a woman named Grace look like, act like? She acted like herself, whoever she was. The same for Gigi.

Except... In my mind, the woman in the pictures was Gigi.

"You're sure you're ready?" Hillary asked.

"To remember? Of course. Madeleine and Smitty both said that breaking the curse requires more knowledge of my past."

"But we know Adele Galloway is the most likely culprit to have cursed you. If you don't want to see..." She made an irritated noise. "If you're not ready to see the place where your girlfriend died, then we'll pursue the mother angle."

The car slowed as she spoke. Hillary probably didn't even realize she'd dropped five miles under the speed limit.

"I'm sure. I need to do this."

Hillary gripped the steering wheel in a death clench, and then we were pulling off the road and onto the shoulder.

Belatedly, I saw it: a roadside memorial about half a football field down the road. Flowers in varying stages of decay or desiccation, a photo, and a cross planted firmly in the ground all marked the site of a young woman's death.

Hillary must have spotted it, and that was why we'd pulled off early. She was giving me a little space. A little time.

So we sat in the car. Her waiting. Me not looking at the memorial.

Eventually I decided it wouldn't get any easier in five minutes or five hours, so better to get it over with it. I debated pushing through the car door—an unpleasant but sometimes necessary method of dealing with inanimate objects in my path—but Hillary predicted my need, hopped out of the driver's seat, and opened my door in record time.

She waited, leaning on the open door, and watched me.

There were too many questions there, and I had no answers. Not yet. My gaze landed on the piles of flowers, the ones I'd so overtly ignored mere minutes before, the ones that now held my complete attention.

Some of them were fresh.

The thud of the car door closing startled me.

"I'm coming with you."

She hadn't posed it as a question, but I agreed nonetheless. "Yes."

It wasn't as if I could keep her away, and saying it aloud helped me to feel more in control.

The road hadn't looked familiar as we'd driven here. My attention had been split between the passing scenery and Grace—Gigi—but I'd kept my eyes out, and nothing had sparked a flash of recognition.

Neither did the memorial site.

I recognized the picture, but only because it had been on the memorial website. Whoever had chosen it had made an odd choice. It wasn't the happiest or the prettiest picture. Gigi sat in a swing that hung from a tree, and she looked off into the distance rather than at the photographer. It had been the most subdued of the pictures on the site.

I took a step closer to the photo, intending to, I don't know, pick it up? Look at it more closely, check for an inscription?

But my legs wobbled and wouldn't support me. I fell to my knees, astonished at first by my body's failure to cooperate. I'd been without substance for over three years, but my body had always worked.

But then the pain hit me.

Sharp. Needles, knives, and hacksaw sharp.

It pushed into my brain, tearing, ripping, shredding. I reached for my head, expecting a wet, bloody mess, but only felt my hair.

I struggled to stand. I felt vulnerable kneeling, but the pain kept pushing. Into my head. Into my mind.

And then I staggered as the edges of my vision narrowed. A brief moment of panic, of utter vulnerability to the thing attacking me, hit me, and then…nothing.

21

HILLARY

The horror of watching someone I cared about crumple into a motionless heap was chilling.

Literally. I stood shivering for...I wasn't sure how long. Too long. Terrible thoughts tumbled through my head.

Some part of my mind started to work, and I realized I didn't have time to be helpless and confused. Brad needed my help. I yanked out my phone and started to dial 911, except that was a terrible idea. Shoving my phone in my pocket, I fell to my knees next to him.

Clenching my hands together to keep from trying to touch him, I took a breath. I needed to sound calm. I could do that. I could.

"Can you hear me?"

A moan was my response. That pained sound hurt my heart.

"Can I do anything?" I reached out—I couldn't stop myself—but all I felt was cold and a thickening of the air.

That wasn't at all what it felt like before when we'd come into contact. There were no tingles and certainly no warmth.

His eyelids flickered, and he pulled his eyes open. He squinted as if the sunlight was painful. He tried to answer, but no words came out. A grumbly, frustrated noise was all that he could manage.

My phone was still clutched in my hand. Emergency services might be useless, but I did know one person who might—just maybe—be able to help.

She answered on the second ring. "Every Woman's Fairy Godmother. How can I help you?"

"Madeleine!" My eyes stung, and I had to fight the overwhelming urge to sob. If I hiccuped and cried, she wouldn't be able to understand a word. She needed to understand, and she needed to help me. In a much calmer tone, I said, "I need your help. Please help me."

"What can I do?"

Her quiet calm gave me the reassurance I'd desperately needed. I relayed what had happened and waited.

"He's fine."

"He's not fine." I was looking at him. He wasn't fine.

"He's probably fine."

"Do you want me to send you a picture? He's on the ground, incapable of speech, and clearly in a *lot* of pain."

"Can he hear you?"

I'd looked away as I spoke with Madeleine. I couldn't look at Brad, suffering like he was, and hold a rational conversation. I put my phone on speaker and dropped it to the ground, then turned to Brad.

"Honey, can you hear me? Blink if you can hear me."

He'd closed his eyes again, so it was hard to see, but he squeezed his closed eyes tighter.

"Hang on. I'm trying to get help. You're going to be okay. Madeleine said so, and I'm sure she's right." I was babbling, so I shut up and picked up my phone again. I didn't want Brad to hear whatever Madeleine had to say...just in case. Tapping the speaker off, I said, "He can hear me, but he really isn't doing well."

"Ask him if he remembers."

"Remembers what?"

She paused, and some shuffling in the background was followed by the distinct click of a door shutting. "Everything, Hillary."

Oh. Oh my. What if all those memories were

being shoved back in his head right now? That sounded... Good grief.

"Brad, sweetie, blink if you're starting to remember anything."

He squeezed his eyes shut—once, twice, three times. Either that meant no, or emphatically yes.

"I think he's saying yes."

"Hillary, listen to me. Your trip to the crash site must have broken the memory portion of the curse. Brad's getting his memory back, and it's not an easy process. But it won't, um, *shouldn't* damage him."

I might have a heart attack right here, right now. *Shouldn't damage him?*

"Are you listening to me, Hillary? Tell him it's going to be okay, and it will be over soon."

Hanging up wasn't the most brilliant idea, but that didn't occur to me until after I'd done it. Calm Brad. Keep him company, tell him everything would be okay, that was what I was doing.

All the questions I had for Madeleine fled once she told me what was happening and that we just had to wait it out.

I sat down cross-legged next to him.

"You're okay. I know it feels really terrible, but you're okay. You'll be okay. I talked to Madeleine, and she said so. She's my fairy godmother, so she has to know stuff like that." And I babbled on in that vein for several minutes: everything was going to be fine, we just had to wait it out, and, naturally, Madeleine would know, because it was her job to know.

Did I believe any of it? Nope.

And I went on not believing any of it, right up until Fate (the evil wench) patted me on the back and told me I was right to be wary.

Because Brad was not okay. He wasn't fine at all.

He was gone.

One minute, my heart was being squished like a bug because I had to sit and watch him suffer, unable to do anything to make it better.

The next, he was gone.

22

HILLARY

"Maybe he's just invisible. To me. Invisible to me. I'm sure Gramps can still see him." I was speaking to thin air as I drove not as safely as I should to my grandfather's house.

Talking nonsense to myself as I sped down the road was wacked. Nuttier than talking to Gramps' imaginary friend...because Brad was real, so that wasn't strange at all.

Just because he'd disappeared into thin air didn't mean he'd never existed.

It also didn't mean he was gone. He was still there, invisible to me but there.

He had to be.

Gosh, he was probably upset I'd driven off and left him.

No need to dwell on the unanswered questions I'd shouted into the air at Grace's memorial site. ("Where are you? Are you still here? Give me a sign that you can hear me.") Or the fact that I'd gone on and on with various versions of the same questions and demands that Brad make himself known to me for, oh, probably a good hour.

Not crazy at all.

I'd kept it up until a kind woman pulled over to ask if I'd lost my dog. Apparently, I'd looked like a distressed pet owner calling out for Fluffy by the roadside.

Since I didn't need to be carted away in a straitjacket, I agreed with the nice lady that I had lost my dog (I know, I'm a terrible human being), but declined her help. Then I promptly left for Gramps' with a side trip to my place to pick up a particularly sparkly pair of glasses I'd left there.

I zipped into his driveway and screeched to a halt. Not that my tires actually screeched. I wasn't driving like a panicked sixteen-year-old. I was driving like a panicked twenty-eight-year-old, because I *was* a panicked twenty-eight-year-old.

Brad could be in purgatory.

He could be invisible to everyone, including me and Gramps.

He could have been transported to some other place, like when Madeleine saved him from purgatory. (I'd called her twenty times—no exaggeration—to ask, but she wasn't answering.)

What if I never saw him again?

What if... What if he was dead?

A tap on my window made me scream.

Uh-huh. I screamed like a little girl watching a horror flick after midnight when her brother grabs her shoulder from behind. Brothers suck.

Sneaky grandpas were a little annoying, too.

I rolled my window down. "Get in. We have to go find Brad."

Without argument, Gramps walked around the front of my Fiat and then climbed into the passenger seat.

I backed out and considered my options. I'd leave out the dead possibility, for sure. I'd also skip purgatory. Probably best to stick to basic facts. "I'm not sure why, but I can't see Brad anymore."

"When did that happen?" He sounded a heck of a lot calmer than me.

"We went to Grace's—sorry, Gigi's—roadside memorial. Well, we didn't know it was going to be a memorial. We went to the place where the car crash happened, and there was a memorial there." I chewed on my lower lip. "That was about an hour and a half, two hours ago."

"Hm. Any reason you left the old man at home?"

"Hey, I could barely get Brad to agree to take *me*. He didn't think it was safe."

Gramps pondered that for a minute or so, then said, "Might not have been. Could be that if you can't see him, it's because he's not there."

He'd clearly gone through at least some of the permutations I'd skipped over: purgatory, magically transported...dead.

"He hasn't left." Gramps squeezed my forearm. "Not like you're thinking."

I considered my words carefully as I drove at a moderate pace. There was no reason to upset my grandfather, and speeding or verbalizing my panicked fears would do that.

One person who was about to lose her marbles was enough. Then again, maybe he knew something I didn't?

"How do you know? He was there, and then he was just...gone. He disappeared right in front of me, Gramps. And Madeleine thinks he might have gotten his memory back." No need to go into the details of why my FG thought that, or how terrifying it had been to witness Brad's debilitating pain. "Maybe regaining his memory triggered the end of the curse? You know, an end that someone who cursed people would be happy with."

"He's not dead."

I huffed out an exasperated breath.

"Peanut, have a little faith. Someone out there, maybe Brad's fairy godmother, maybe mine, maybe someone else entirely, lent Brad and I a helping hand. Someone put us in each other's path when we most needed a friend."

My peevish previous thoughts about Fate aside (and yes, she was an evil wench), I didn't usually put much stock in that lady's guiding hand. Gramps didn't typically either, but of the two of us, I was the one more likely to believe in the power of the unexplainable.

Heck, I consulted a psychic—aura reader, whatever—on the regular.

I had a fairy godmother, for goodness' sake.

And yet here he was, trying to convince me to have a little faith.

Well, pfft. That was what I had to say to having a little faith. Madeleine wasn't reachable by phone. Mary Margaret was a gem, but she'd done everything she could. And Smitty, while he'd definitely come through for us, wasn't much help at this juncture.

And whoever created the BFF team of Walter and Brad, if there was even such a person, didn't seem to be around right now.

My best hope was that Brad would still be visible to Gramps. That whatever Madeleine had done to my sunglasses would work again. That somehow, someway, Gramps and I would pull off the road next to a certain memorial and Brad would be waiting for us.

Seven minutes later, I pulled off the road onto the shoulder.

Brad was not waiting for us.

"Try the glasses," Gramps said after he'd scanned the area.

He was reaching for the door handle when I stopped him with a surprising admission: "I like him."

"I know."

Okay, then. Maybe not so surprising. Not to Gramps. It was to me. Because when I said "I like him," what I really meant was that I *like* liked him.

I cared about Brad in a way that was unexpected after only a few days. Unexpected and unpleasant. I wasn't ready for love. I was busy. I had businesses to run. Clients to make happy. Life goals to achieve.

And love was hard.

Not that I was in love. I wasn't. Except I was maybe in pre-love. The falling part. Maybe.

Except love led to relationships.

And relationships were hard.

Relationships took work and commitment and... And commitment.

And two hours ago, the guy I might be falling for had no body. Right this very minute, he might be so many particles in the ether or in purgatory, wherever that was. I was pretty sure, wherever it was, that I couldn't visit.

"Sweet pea, you've got to pull it together."

I peeled my cramping fingers away from the tortured steering wheel of my Fiat, then sent Sophia a silent apology for abusing her lovely car self. I forced a grim smile. "I'm together."

"You're not together. You're a mess, peanut. And I understand, because I'm worried, too. But we have to keep it together and do the next thing."

I cocked my head. "What next thing?"

He patted my knee. "Breathe."

His words spurred a deep inhalation, one that made me realize how oxygen-deprived I'd been, sitting here, worrying about Brad, worrying about me, worrying about me and Brad.

Wow, was I being selfish. Brad was Gramps' best friend. They were so BFF that I wanted to give them a couple name. Bralter. Yeah, that wasn't happening. Also, they weren't dating, so that would be super weird.

"Breathe," Gramps reminded me again.

So I did. A few times, deeply. I even remembered the exhaling part.

"Now put your glasses on and have a look around."

I pointed at him. "Good plan. You have this

thinking-under-stress thing nailed, Gramps. Have I told you lately I love you?"

He cracked a smile, a genuine one, unlike the weak imitation I'd given him earlier. "I love you too, peanut. Now put your glasses on."

Wearing my magicked glasses, I scanned both sides of the road. "I don't see him."

"Let's get out, walk around a little, make sure he's not here, and..." Gramps trailed off, because the only way Brad would be here and visible without us having already spotted him was if he was prone on the ground. "Let's just double-check."

After we'd both exited the car, Gramps said, "And when we're done, you're giving me that Madeleine's phone number. With the fancy caller ID on phones, she has to know it's you calling. Maybe she's ducking your calls."

I shook my head and tried to entertain myself envisioning a call where Gramps got hold of Madeleine after I'd failed to. I was pretty sure he'd read her the riot act. One did not duck calls, according to my grandfather. It had taken a while for him to accept that spammers didn't count as "people," and so it wasn't a violation of polite behavior to refuse to answer those calls.

Mostly I was looking at the ground, hoping I wouldn't find Brad there.

But the Gramps-Madeleine phone scenario was

a solid effort on my part to keep my blood pressure from spiking every time I saw the shadow of a log or a dip in the terrain.

Eventually, Gramps and I had to call our search unsuccessful. We'd covered the small area at least three times.

Gramps tried calling Madeleine from his phone, but she didn't pick up for him, either.

When he ended the unsuccessful call, he looked at me for several seconds. "Let's go home. We'll try again in the morning."

I nodded my agreement, but I had no hope we'd find Brad in the morning. He wasn't here, and a few hours of restless sleep wouldn't change that.

Gramps drove.

I cried.

23

BRAD

Some new hell had been visited upon me.

I'd regained my memory, but I'd lost my friends.

My best friend and my...Hillary.

I'd jumped up and down, yelled, but they'd neither seen nor heard me. I'd even stuck a hand through Walter's back—trying to tap him on the shoulder—but whatever small amount of substance my ghostly form had previously possessed had vaporized. I was completely insubstantial now.

I was also stuck.

When Walter and Hillary left, I'd tried to follow them. I understood why they'd left. I wasn't upset or surprised by their departure. They couldn't see or hear me, so it was reasonable to assume I was no longer present.

But I was present—and trapped in a bubble the size of a three-car garage, with Gigi's memorial at the center.

It wasn't a force field or a wall. I just couldn't walk past a certain point.

Eventually, I stopped trying. I dropped to the grass on the opposite side of the road from Gigi's memorial. I wasn't hiding from her pictures or trying to escape the weight of the cross and the flowers. I just needed a little space, and that was best found on the opposite side of the road.

Daylight turned to dusk, then dusk to dark.

Sitting in the blackness of night on a road that was rarely traveled, I fell into a contemplative state similar to what I imagined meditation produced. I wasn't the kind of guy to meditate, so I was definitely guessing.

And I *knew* that I didn't meditate. I also knew that I liked my whiskey on the rocks, my steak medium, and my workouts strenuous. I'd been a physical guy. I ran. I swam. I played football through high school, baseball through my sophomore year of college, and had started to play hockey after moving to Minnesota.

After Gigi.

Whoever had cursed me—and I was fairly confident of the culprit—they'd known me well enough to know that being without a body would be its own kind of torture. They'd also known that being isolated from humanity would devastate me.

She'd been trying to drive me mad.

Adele Galloway, Gigi's mother.

What happened the night of Gigi's death had been an accident. Terrible, tragic, heartrending—but an accident.

It had taken me a year of self-hatred, grief, guilt, and intensive counseling to come to terms with the fact that I hadn't been responsible. As the anniversary of Gigi's death had neared, I'd felt a need to say goodbye. That was why I'd been in Austin over three years ago.

I would always miss Gigi. Always.

But that awful weight I'd felt the last several years hadn't really been mine. That had been a part of the curse, because in my heart I no longer carried that terrible burden.

I stood up, thankful for the light of the almost-full moon. My eyes had adjusted to the darkness, but for what I wanted to do, I needed some light.

I crossed the street and walked toward Gigi's memorial. The cross supported a picture, and that was my destination.

As I neared, I felt the familiar tug of loss. The welling of sadness that I suspected wouldn't ever completely disappear.

She'd been beautiful. Not a girl with a perfect

figure or flawless skin or the even features seen in the movies. She'd been bright and funny and generous, and all those wonderful qualities had shone through. She'd had presence. Her vitality and charm had been infectious.

To know Gigi was to fall a little in love with her.

Her mother had adored her.

Gigi had tolerated Adele's overprotective nature. She'd laughed at her mother's inability to accept her friends or her career choice. Nothing and no one were good enough for Adele's darling child.

Adele had despised me, naturally. How could she not? I was her daughter's wicked despoiler. The first boy who'd captured Gigi's attention, and eventually the man she'd considered marrying.

We hadn't been engaged, but we'd been close, and Adele had hated that.

Some of Adele's disapproval might have stemmed from differences I'd been completely unaware of at the time. But even if I'd had magic or known about a world filled with curses and fairy godmothers, I had no chance at Adele's approval.

Maybe I hadn't been good enough for Gigi. But I'd loved her the best way I knew how. In my youth and inexperience, I might not always have made the best choices—but I'd loved my girl. More importantly, she'd felt loved, and she'd been happy.

But that had never been enough for Adele.

In retrospect, it shouldn't come as any great shock that Adele was a witch. Gigi's mom fit the stereotypical evil witch role all too well.

I knelt in front of the cross and picture. I remembered it. I'd actually taken it.

Gigi's father—another man Adele had held in contempt—died a few days before I'd snapped the photo. Gigi and her father hadn't been close, but she'd been unprepared for the loss and taken it hard.

Such an odd choice for a memorial. There was nothing of Gigi's happy, carefree nature in the picture, very little of Gigi in it at all, except the grief she'd been feeling in that moment.

Also, *I'd* taken the picture.

The man Adele believed responsible for the death of her beloved child.

But I knew the truth. The restoration of my memory made that possible.

Gigi had died in an accident I had been unable to prevent. I hadn't been intoxicated, tired, distracted, or inattentive. It had been, in every sense of the word, an accident.

I'd loved her in every way I'd known how.

We'd been happy. *She'd* been happy. Happy in her career, with our lives together, and with the adventures she'd believed waited just around the corner.

As all of those thoughts swirled in my head, a few pieces of the curse's puzzle fit together.

Adele must have known I was taking the first steps in moving past Gigi's death. Somehow, she knew I'd released the terrible guilt I'd been feeling—and she'd been furious.

Plant the guilt she believed I deserved. Take away my memories so I couldn't work my way through it. Give me no substance, so the physical outlets I normally used to cope with stress were no longer available to me.

And, for the final touch of torture, make me unknowable. Silenced and invisible, I would have been unable to create the connections I so desperately needed with other human beings for my mental well-being. I wasn't a loner. I was a joiner. I'd played team sports my whole life, I'd dated my high school sweetheart through college and beyond, and I adored my mother.

The people who were dear to me kept me grounded during Gigi's death. They'd kept me sane.

And Adele didn't want me sane. She wanted me to suffer in every way possible.

All of that was a pretty nasty conclusion to reach. As a guy who made friends easily and liked people, it bothered me to have someone out in the world who despised me.

It more than bothered me when that person actively worked to ruin my life.

It was a lot to digest...but it seemed I had time.

I couldn't leave, so I settled in to wait.

I wasn't completely without options though.

Wait and panic. Wait and worry. Wait and plot.

Those were the choices available to me, and I knew which I had to choose.

24

HILLARY

I slept.

There was some more crying, some serious anxiety, and Gramps definitely stayed over for the night—but I did eventually fall asleep.

When I woke the next morning, I experienced about point two seconds of a lethargic, slow-waking, normal morning. That fraction of a second was glorious, mostly in comparison to what followed: the truth of my life revealed.

It sounds melodramatic. It wasn't, actually. I just figured out a few things that had been staring me in the face for a while now.

Friends, family, basically anyone who cared about me, had been telling me the same things. I worked too much. I didn't make time for a personal life. I needed to focus on one business and sell the rest or hire employees. I needed to commit to my future rather than dabble.

That last was my mother. She said I dabbled at life, love, and business.

My crazy realization this morning? She wasn't entirely wrong.

As with many things to do with my mother, she also wasn't entirely right—but I got her point. I got it now, because I'd found something...someone who required more of me than dabbling.

Or maybe it was a truer statement to say that I required more of me than dabbling, because I was falling. Head first, inelegantly, and with all my heart.

Darn Madeleine and her stupid glasses and her silly "possibility of love," because I was feeling the possibilities in bed that morning.

Not *that* kind of possibility.

Not *only* that kind of possibility.

I'd been thinking more of the emotional connection Brad and I had established over the last few days. My throat burned, because I had an emotional connection with—real talk, I was *falling in love with*—a guy who was at best cursed to a life with no physical presence on this earth. At worst, he was gone, banished to purgatory or maybe even dead.

And now I was going to cry again.

That point two seconds of emotional calm I'd

experienced this morning sure did look good from where I was right now.

Gramps knocked on my door. "You awake in there, peanut?"

I pulled a pillow over my head, fully prepared to pretend that I wasn't. That "knowing is half the battle" crap is such garbage.

Given the revelations of the morning, I knew I needed to sell at least two of my baby businesses, so the others could flourish and grow into adulthood.

I knew I needed to make time in my life for friends, family (not just Gramps), and love.

And I knew that love had planted its insidious seed in my heart, probably when Gramps had started to tell stories about Brad, the amazing man he was and the impact he'd had on Gramps' life. That seed had taken root, likely when I'd seen the man himself and realized he wasn't the figment of a lonely widower's imagination. And now it was trying really, really hard to grow, even though Brad was AWOL.

Knowing was *not* half the battle. I felt overwhelmed and angry with Fate (evil wench), and kinda pissed at my FG for putting me in this position.

My bed dipped. "Wake up. I've got news and a plan."

I shoved the pillow off my head and looked at

Gramps. "Really? Because I've got nothing but a whole lot of depressing thoughts."

"I've had a chat with Smitty and Madeleine."

That perked me up.

Gramps patted my shoulder. "And I have coffee in the kitchen."

I hopped out of bed, shooed Gramps out the door, and was changed and in the kitchen in record time.

I wrapped my fingers around the cute pink mug Gramps had chosen for me. The warmth seeped into my skin and the aroma of well-brewed dark coffee with cream and sugar filled my nose. "Tell me about this plan."

25

HILLARY

Gramps and I headed back to the roadside memorial site.

Smitty, being our ghost and witches (sort of) expert, plumbed his knowledge and came up with a plan last night that he shared with Gramps in the early hours this morning.

That phrase "if all you have is a hammer, everything looks like a nail" definitely applied here, because Smitty wanted to use a ghost to solve our witch's curse problem.

Maybe it made sense? But maybe it was just Smitty piecing together the only knowledge he had to try and help us.

On the upside, we did have a plan. Not necessarily a *good* plan, but some action that might bring us closer to our goal of saving Brad. Gosh, and I guess Gramps, too. I'd forgotten all about my grandfather's psych eval and housing dilemma in the last twenty-four hours. It seemed my brain could only handle the crisis directly in front of it. Gramps' problem had gotten shelved as soon as Brad's situation had blown up.

Sorry, brain. Just keep it together a little while longer...

I kept my eyes on the road, as I prepared to grill Gramps. I'd insisted on driving. More as proof to myself that I wasn't a wreck than for any other reason. That was me, keeping it together.

"Summoning a dead person's spirit sounds risky. Madeleine was sure there's no way this could hurt Brad? He won't get sucked into some otherworldly vortex?" At least we had Madeleine's expertise going for us. Smitty had come up with the broad strokes of the plan, but Madeleine had provided the magical details, specifically, the summoning ritual.

"She says Brad won't be affected. We just have to follow the instructions carefully to be sure we don't invite the wrong person to visit."

"The wrong person to visit?" I repeated, because...who? Some random dead person who happened to have died in the vicinity of Gigi's memorial was gonna pop in and say hello?

"Don't look so panicked. If we follow the instructions, it'll be fine."

"And Madeleine thought Smitty's plan was solid?"

Gramps hesitated, one of his many tells, and then said, "Madeleine thought his reasoning that Gigi was at the heart of Adele's curse was sound. Oh, and she did confirm that Adele is a witch. I guess there's something like a yellow pages for witches. She looked up the Galloway family, and Adele and Gigi were both in there."

Of course there was a witch directory. Why wouldn't there be? Once you got past matchmaking fairy godmothers, nothing else was much of a leap.

But back to the plan, because my brain really liked that there was a plan. Having a plan almost made it happy. "So, to recap, we summon Gigi, which should work because we have an FG-approved ritual. Then we ask her to get in touch with her mom."

"If she can understand us and communicate."

I squeezed out my frustration on my poor little Fiat's steering wheel. "Do ghosts not communicate well?"

"Smitty was a little vague about that part."

I cleared my throat and continued. "Right, so we summon Gigi, hope she can have a conversation, ask her to put in a good word with her mom, and then...?"

"Then we send her back."

"Uh-huh." I flicked my blinker on. The turn to the county road where the accident had taken place was coming up. "You do know this whole thing sounds half-baked."

"I am aware, yes." He sent me a gentle smile. "But it got you out of bed this morning."

My heart swelled with love for the kind-hearted man sitting next to me. "Fair point. Do we have the ritual to send Gigi back?"

Gramps patted his breast pocket. The piece of paper tucked inside crinkled with the momentary pressure.

"Uh-huh. Any word from Smitty?" Our post shop owner/paranormal investigator had been looking for a last-minute sub when Gramps and I had left the house. Smitty was scheduled to work at the shop this morning, and he couldn't exactly shut the place down to help us with a ghost summoning.

"Just two texts complaining that his staff have no sense of humor or adventure, and that he clearly paid them too much since three had turned down triple pay to fill in for him."

Aw. Poor Smitty. He really didn't want to miss out. Also, poor me; I wouldn't mind the backup.

Madeleine made it clear she wasn't allowed to attend our summoning. She also implied that we'd discovered the ritual on our own, should anyone happen to ask.

No Smitty. No Madeleine. Just Gramps, me, and a ghost. Good times.

"We've got this, peanut." He patted my knee.

We did.

Not really, but if I said it in my head enough, maybe it would come true. The power of positive thinking. Fake it till you make it. Courage before comfort.

Nope. Not helping. My hands were shaking as I pulled onto the shoulder in front of the memorial.

Gramps and I both scanned the area, because maybe... But I didn't see any signs of Brad, and Gramps shook his head.

While Gramps retrieved the small box of supplies we'd need for the ritual from Sophia's cargo area, I grabbed a blanket from the backseat and looked for an even spot in the grass. I didn't know how long ghost summonings took, but just in case it was a flop or we had to wait around a while, it seemed like a good idea.

As Gramps approached, I spotted a bottle of champagne peeking out of the box. "Did you snag a bottle of bubbly for me or the ghost?"

"The ghost. I don't think either of us should be imbibing." He set the box between us, then planted himself on the blanket. "If one shouldn't operate heavy equipment while under the influence, then opening a connection to the spirit world probably isn't a good idea either."

I'd been kidding, but it looked like our ghost was going to get the benefit of an expensive bottle of champagne I'd been hoarding for just the right occasion. I couldn't think of anything better. If a little fizzy wine furthered Brad's cause, then Gigi could have all the champagne. I eyed the bottles Gramps was retrieving from the box. Gigi could have all the champagne, all the tequila, and all the vodka that she liked.

There was an absence of whiskey, and I know I had some at the house.

"Are you saving the whiskey for yourself, Gramps?"

He frowned. "No. We're supposed to make her feel welcome, so I picked the drinks I thought she'd like." I cocked an eyebrow, and he rolled his eyes. "Don't tell me. Ladies like whiskey, too. You know you only drink it when I don't have anything else."

I wasn't arguing about whiskey and equality right now. I held out my hand. "Let me see this ritual."

He retrieved the piece of paper, handed it over, then unpacked the remainder of our supplies.

I stopped mid-scan when I realized everything he was unloading. "You brought my prosciutto?

Really, Gramps? Is that supposed to make Gigi feel welcome?"

"Nope. She was a vegetarian. That's for me." He snatched the packet of deliciousness with a guilty look. "I've been up for hours. I need a snack."

Our blanket was looking more like a picnic than anything remotely paranormal. This time when I looked at the instructions, I read them carefully. "Well, that's interesting. A few candles—"

"For ambiance."

I cocked an eyebrow. "Booze." I held up my hand. "I get it, to make Gigi feel welcome. Flowers?"

Gramps pointed at the tiny potted orchid. It wasn't flowering, but it was the only thing remotely resembling flowers at my house.

"Oh, now this is interesting. Salt, sage, rosemary, basil, cinnamon, clove, ginger—" All in my spice cabinet, but—"Lavender? Peppermint and chamomile?"

Gramps pointed to a linen spray and tea bags. "Madeleine said these would be fine. She walked me through a list and told me where to find most of it. By the way, your lavender room spray doesn't have any lavender in it."

But apparently my linen spray did. This was too bizarre.

"It's a lot of odds and ends. Do we make some kind of mix with it?"

He was spreading the herbs and the contents of the tea bags all around the edges of the blanket. "I don't know what this stuff does. Madeleine said we were stacking the deck in our favor. That she didn't have time to explain how everything should be properly used."

So now we had a spice fest happening around us that might or might not aid in summoning the dead girlfriend of the man I was falling in love with, who happened to be in the wind.

Oh, Lord. I hoped he wasn't really in the wind. As in, completely insubstantial and as one with the wind.

"Hillary?"

I blinked and everything around me came back into focus. Gramps had lit the three small candles and placed them in a triangular shape, two at the blanket's corners and the third along the opposite edge. We'd ended up with a triangle of candles inside a square of salt, herbs, and tea, and inside that we had a glass each of vodka, tequila, and champagne, and my little orchid. And no prosciutto. Gramps must have polished it off.

If we didn't all end up in flames, we'd be lucky. Those herbs were all flammable and Gramps hadn't brought candle holders.

"What's next?" Gramps indicated the paper I'd forgotten I was holding.

I smoothed it out and started to read aloud the foreign words written underneath the preparation instructions. I paused to remind Gramps that we're supposed to be thinking welcoming thoughts, and before I began again, I noticed a gentle breeze had started to blow.

"Keep reading," Gramps said. "You're not supposed to stop."

Following his instruction, I continued to read the words written in no language I recognized. If Gramps hadn't warned me otherwise, the steadily increasing wind would have stopped me, but I forged ahead.

I carefully sounded out each of the words, until I came to the end. The very last words were the easiest, because these were words I knew.

"Grace Galloway."

26

BRAD

Watching Hillary and Walter was painful.

Especially Hillary. She looked tired and pale. It had been less than a day, but she had dark smudges under her eyes and a drawn, pinched appearance that made my gut twist.

But then she and Walter set up...a picnic?

Blanket, check. Adult beverages, check. A potted plant? Weird, but check.

Yeah, that looked like a picnic to me.

While I was lost to human contact and wondering if I'd ever be able to touch the woman who'd found her way into my heart, they were picnicking. Was that prosciutto Walter was stuffing into his mouth? Really? I loved that stuff.

And the candles appeared, and then it just got

crazy bizarre. They were sprinkling something all around the blanket.

What in the ever-loving—

But then I saw Hillary consult a scrap of paper and realized I might be witnessing the unfolding of a plan.

Something had kept me from approaching as they'd unpacked—perhaps the creep factor?—but now that I suspected magical shenanigans were afoot, I closed the distance.

That's when Hillary started to read from the piece of paper. The words came out slowly and awkwardly in a tongue completely unfamiliar to me. I spoke a little German, Italian, and Russian, and whatever Hillary was reading didn't remotely resemble any of those languages. I peeked over her shoulder to make sure it wasn't her pronunciation that was throwing me off, and it wasn't.

Then the wind picked up. If I'd been worried about the creepy factor earlier, I shouldn't have. Midmorning, sunny and still, there hadn't been a hint of a breeze. Then the creepy words, followed by the creepy breeze, followed by the even creepier wind.

By the time she stopped—and the end was hard to miss, since it was Gigi's name—the wind was gusting. Hillary's hair whipped around her face, tangling in her mouth.

She scraped all the bright strands together and made a sort of ponytail bun, which distracted me because I loved her hair. Because of that momentary diversion, I failed to see Gigi's entrance.

But Gigi was here.

Not as I had last seen her, broken, bloody and still. She appeared as she'd been in life. Vibrant. Beautiful. Whole.

She could see me. I knew she could, because our eyes met and held for several seconds. It was… odd. I felt all the love for her I'd always felt, but there was a distance between me and those feelings. I blinked and the connection between us was lost.

I suspected the distance I felt was her death. Or grief survived. Or time. Maybe all of those things.

The sight of her stirred some of the less pleasant emotions I'd experienced in the wake of her loss. How alone I'd felt; she'd been my best friend for years. How sad; her life had been cut so horribly short. And I felt just the smallest hint of shame; because I'd moved on. I was falling in love with another woman, and that woman was standing just a few feet away.

She'd never been the kind to judge, and I doubted she was now. It had been four years after all.

And she wasn't here for me. When we broke eye

contact, her attention shifted to Walter, then Hillary, where it remained. "You called me?"

Hillary opened her mouth to reply; nonsense emerged. "Thank goodness. I thought we might have to use sign language, except I don't know sign language, and we don't have a Ouija board or anything like that. We really weren't at all prepared, and especially not for communication difficulties, because I didn't even know that was a problem until we were already on the way. And... Yay! You can understand us."

A smile tugged at my lips. My sweet girl was nervous. She did tend to babble when she was anxious.

Gigi laughed. The throaty sound reassured me even more than her appearance that she was the woman I'd known four years ago. My Gigi had always had a sense of humor, and even if she wasn't mine any longer, she was still that woman I'd known all those years ago.

"Some ghosts pretend they can't hear or speak." She tilted her head to the side, a simple movement that was incredibly familiar. "Some can't, but most can."

"It solves so many problems that we can talk to you. It's a huge relief. And a surprise. Also, that you're..." Hillary lifted her hands, a little like she was framing Gigi for a picture.

"Solid," Walter said. "You're very solid, not like a ghost."

"Oh," Gigi said with surprise. Then she stepped forward and extended her hand in a belated offer of greeting. "I'm Gigi, your friendly corporeal ghost. I thought you knew that since you summoned me."

Walter and Hillary both shook hands with my dead girlfriend while I watched from the sidelines. Surreal? Perhaps, but no more so than being cursed by her witch mother and meeting my current love interest's fairy godmother.

When both Hillary and Walter stood quietly, not quite but almost gaping at her, Gigi said, "I don't have much time. Why did you summon me? Something to do with Brad?"

She glanced over her shoulder at me.

"They can't see me." Until she nodded her understanding, I hadn't been certain she could hear me.

Forced isolation was a whopper of a curse, and after only half a day off the human grid, I was pretty certain I wouldn't last long with no human contacts.

Good grief. I'd probably start haunting Hillary. Talk about the creepiest of the creepy. Just what she needed: a ghostly stalker.

"Right." Hillary lifted her chin. Her determination was adorable. "Long story short, your mom is evil and cursed Brad a year after you died." She paused, then said, "I'm so sorry for your, ah, death." She cleared her throat and continued. "Gramps and I could see him—"

"Three years," Gramps supplied.

"I've only been able to see him a few days," Hillary said calmly, but she blushed. She might be fair, but Hillary was not a blusher. "Anyway, Brad lost his memory when he was cursed, and he also became invisible, basically. No one could see him except me and Gramps. I brought him here to help jog his memory, which turned out to be a bad idea, because he's gone again. Wow, this isn't the short version. Really, really short story: we need you to convince your mom to remove the curse."

"Ah." Gigi gestured to the spread at their feet. "Any chance this was for me?"

Walter nodded. "Can I offer you a drink? We've got tequila, vodka, and champagne." He scratched his jaw. "No whiskey, sorry about that."

"Champagne. I'll have a quick sip before I pop off." She accepted the glass of bubbly, finished half the glass, then said, "Convincing my mother to remove the curse will be difficult." Gigi turned to me. "You'll have to do it."

"Wait, what?" Hillary looked beyond Gigi in my direction. "Is that Brad? Is he here? Please tell me he's here, and I didn't accidentally send him off to purgatory. And if it's my fault because I brought you here yesterday, I'm really sorry, Brad."

Gigi's lips twitched. She always could find humor in any situation. Too bad the catalyst was my cursed fate and Hillary's distress over it...except Hillary stressed out was kind of ridiculously cute.

Not that I would ever say that. She wouldn't appreciate the sentiment.

"He's here." Gigi finished off her glass. "He'll have to make the argument. I can't stay."

Then she set down the glass, walked toward me, leaned close, and whispered in my ear.

Her breath tickled, but the meaning of her words didn't sink in until she stepped away.

"It was lovely to meet you." Her comment was directed at Hillary. She waved at Walter, then me. Finally, she looked out into the distance and called, "Momma."

One word.

That's all she'd needed to summon the evil witch herself.

27

HILLARY

"Momma." That's what Gigi had called Adele.

The woman who'd appeared the exact moment Gigi vanished looked like a "momma." She certainly didn't look like an evil, curse-throwing witch.

Not that I had any knowledge of the local witch power structure, but I'd lay odds Adele Galloway was the wickedest witch in Texas. And yet her appearance was anything but.

Southern soccer mom came to mind.

She wore a pink sundress that revealed toned, tanned legs. A short pastel sweater hugged her trim figure, and she'd paired stylish sandals with the outfit. She couldn't have been more than five foot three, versus Gigi's much more significant height, and her hair was styled in a shiny blonde bob. Her pink lip gloss completed the put-together, innocent, athletic look.

Total soccer mom. Then I made eye contact—and took a step back.

Cold, hard, nasty.

There she was, the wicked witch, and she didn't try to hide the nastiness in her gaze.

"Adele."

I froze. That had been a man's voice, and it wasn't Gramps'. I whirled around to find Brad standing a mere two feet behind me.

"Stephen." Adele's voice dripped with venom.

Gramps, Lord love him, extended his hand. "Walter Barrett, pleasure ma'am."

Please do not take his hand. If you take his hand, please let him have it back. In one piece.

My silent prayer was answered. She didn't take his hand, and I'd swear Brad let out a sigh of relief with me.

Adele failed to acknowledge my presence or Gramps', which was just fine by me. But then she lifted a finger and pointed at Brad, and that wasn't fine. Nope. Not at all.

The woman who likes to curse people should not finger point. That thing was a weapon for all I knew. A French-manicured weapon.

I inched closer to Brad. Not that I could protect him, but the instinct was there.

"That's how little you think of my daughter's memory?" Adele's tone and pointed gaze made it clear "that" meant me, and I was the lowest scum of the earth.

"If you had anything to say about it, I wouldn't have any memory of Gigi at all."

"Grace," Adele snapped, color rising in her cheeks. "My daughter's name is Grace. Gigi is a dog's name."

"And yet it was the one she preferred," Brad murmured quietly. As he spoke, he tucked his hand discreetly under my elbow.

Adele and Brad traded barbs, the content of which eluded me, because Brad was touching me. No, my ovaries weren't melting. I was losing my mind a little bit, because Brad had a body. A real, physical presence in this world.

A presence that he was using to casually shield me from Adele. As he spoke with her, he shuffled me slowly away and behind him. Gramps had also gotten the hint and started to slowly retreat.

Seriously? I wasn't going to fuss, because I didn't want to draw attention, but how was he worried about me and Gramps? He was the one she'd cursed.

"We talked to Gigi." Brad's comment caught my

attention, and I tuned out all my worry and annoyance and focused on what the two were saying.

Adele's hard gaze narrowed.

"She told me two things you might find interesting." Brad paused. "Unless you've spoken with her yourself?"

He seemed pretty darn certain that Adele hadn't had a cozy chat with her daughter.

"Tell me, or I'll skewer this woman's heart with a corkscrew." Adele had dropped the pointing finger schtick at some point, but there she went again, waving her weapon of curses and destruction.

She was a real piece of work. Not that there'd been any doubt before her threat, but the reality of her nastiness was eye-opening. I'd never been in the vicinity of someone who casually threatened extreme violence, and she did it with absolute sincerity.

Psychopath, anyone?

Hm. Or a pissed off magical mama bear.

Brad tugged me another inch closer to him. "I don't think you want to do that. You know what the first thing Gigi said to me was?"

Adele's hand fell to her side. The flare of hope in her eyes made mine burn with a hint of tears. I think I'd hit the nail on the head with the mama bear theory.

One thing that splash of hope told me for sure: Adele may have magic, and she may be a cursing fiend, but what she didn't have was a way to speak to her daughter. For some reason, even though Walter and I had been able, Adele couldn't summon her own child.

Brad started to walk backwards slowly. "The first thing she told me? She told me she approves. Of Hillary, of us." He tipped his head toward me when he said "us."

There was an us? My heart beat a happy jig in my chest that Brad thought so.

The seed of love that had been planted in my heart, the one I'd begun to believe was starting to grow? Pretty sure it just had a growth spurt. I was feeling all sorts of warm feelings right now, and none of them had to do with the hard press of Brad's very real body against my own.

Okay, that was obviously a lie. But the attraction was only one feeling amongst many other, not-all-about-sex feelings.

The heightened color in Adele's face leached away, leaving her frighteningly pale.

Right, she'd heard that her daughter's most important message had to do with her boyfriend's love life and not her own mother. Yeah, that was rough.

But I had to give a mental shout out to Gigi. She

wanted her honey to know it was okay that he'd moved on. She was so sweet.

Which made me happy that she'd been in Brad's life, then sad that she'd died and left him alone, and even sadder that her mom had cursed him, then happy that he'd landed here with me, and extra happy that Gigi thought I was the bee's knees. Wow. A lot of emotions were swirling.

Also fear. Fear was swirling.

Because Adele was *pissed*.

Adele's nostrils flared, and she started toward me again. I just knew that hand was going up in another split second.

I wanted to tell her to holster the finger, but from the look on her face I was pretty sure she wouldn't get my nervous brand of humor.

Brad raised his voice. "She also said she forgives you."

Uh-oh.

Not sure what Brad's plan was, but that didn't seem like a good way to go. Giving the trigger-happy angry witch lady another reason to curse us would have been last on my list. Because telling a lady her kid forgives her implies there were hard feelings, ill will, some contention between the two.

Not something to point out in a high stress situation.

I waited for the finger of doom to find its way to

us. Would she curse Brad again? Because it was seeming like he wasn't especially cursed right now. Or maybe me? Or Gramps? I shared a nervous look with Gramps. His eyes were wide, but he didn't seem nearly as worried as me.

Adele deflated like a cheap two-day-old party balloon. Just like that, as fast as a snap of the fingers, she went from avenging angel soccer mom to old, tired, and terribly, terribly sad.

Then the men in my life stepped up.

Brad quietly said, "I'm so sorry for your loss."

And Gramps offered her a hanky.

That's right, the wicked witch of Texas was crying. Not dab-the-corners-of-your-eyes crying. She was ugly crying.

She didn't take the handkerchief. She stared at it and cried even harder. There was snot and hiccuping. And my grandfather, who was the kindest, gentlest man I've ever known, pocketed that hanky and then wrapped Adele in his arms. He tucked her head against his chest, and he held her while she cried out four years of grief denied.

The minutes ticked by, but none of us were in a hurry.

We got odd looks from inside a passing car or two, but who cared?

Eventually, Adele stepped away from Gramps,

and when he offered her his hanky a second time, she took it.

She turned away and tried to make herself presentable.

Not that she should bother. No mascara was living through that tsunami of tears.

When she pivoted to face us, her body was tense. "I made her choose."

Brad shook his head, as stumped as I was.

She lifted her chin, and in that moment, face bare of make-up, eyes puffy and red, she looked so proud, so regal, she could have passed for royalty even with ravages of her grief evident on her face. "You weren't good enough for her."

Brad didn't argue. How could he? Was any man ever good enough for the beloved daughter of a powerful woman?

Maybe, somewhere in time, but the bar was high.

He did say that she was happy.

Adele bit her lip and dipped her chin once in grudging assent. "I made her choose, and she chose you."

Her eyes welled again, but no tears fell.

Brad simply repeated what he'd said before with all the kindness of a man with a generous heart. Mary Margaret had nailed that one. "I'm so very sorry for your loss."

She nodded once more, and then she was gone.

28

BRAD

The moment Adele vanished, I reached for Hillary's hand, spun her toward me, and kissed her.

I was a gentleman—mostly. Walter was standing right there, after all, and I respected him too much to grope his granddaughter in his presence (much).

But I couldn't *not* touch her. I couldn't *not* kiss her. I couldn't *not* cradle her head with one hand and run the other down her back.

The feel of her fiery locks slipping through my fingers was unreal.

The satiny press of her lips against mine was torture, but only because it had to end.

"Just checking," I muttered against her lips.

She leaned away from me just enough to look into my eyes. "Checking what?"

"Making sure I'm really here. That *all* of me is really here."

Walter cleared his throat. "If you've checked enough, maybe we can get this show on the road."

While I'd been having my way with his favorite grandchild, Walter had packed the summoning picnic into a box. He stood waiting, the cardboard box gripped in his age-spotted hands.

With a chaste peck to her lips, I let Hillary go. Then I took the box from Walter, set it on the ground and offered him my hand.

If I didn't know the old guy better, I'd say his eyes were a little shiny when he gripped my fingers. A quick shake and then he pulled me into a hug.

My dad died when I was kid, and I missed out on having a father as a grown man. Walter and I would never have that kind of relationship, because we'd begun as friends and I expected us to continue as friends. But as he hugged me, he felt like family.

Fat drops of rain fell from the sky, putting an end to the moment. The three of us made a mad dash to the car, where we then sat in complete silence.

Once the sound of our breathing had evened, Hillary voiced the question on all our minds, "What now?"

From the backseat, I considered the question. I knew what was next for me. My mother had waited over three years to know what had happened to her son. I needed to see her, talk to her, let her know I was alive, and somehow, someway, explain that I hadn't simply walked away from my life and from her.

"I need to see my mom."

Hillary squared her shoulders. "Yes. Now?"

She left the real question unasked. Was I ready to have a difficult conversation with my mother? Emotionally difficult, because I'd have to convince her my absence wasn't voluntary. And philosophically difficult, because magic played a role in that explanation.

"Now."

29

HILLARY

Gramps and I waited in the car. We couldn't, wouldn't, intrude on Brad's reunion with his mother.

"Not what you expected?" Gramps asked.

"Hm?" I'd been lost in my thoughts, mostly to do with the question of the moment: what now?

"You've been staring at the brick façade on this house for almost ten minutes. I was just asking if Brad's house wasn't what you expected."

I didn't bother to answer the question, because Gramps knew darn well that wasn't what was on my mind.

"I'm going to start inviting guests to appear on my fashion blog." I hadn't even been thinking about my blog, but out the words came.

"Yeah?"

"Uh-huh. And hire an assistant to coordinate the posts." That seemed like a good idea. And maybe I could use that same assistant to tighten up my personal shopping schedule. Maybe even coordinate other things...other people. "You know, I think I know a few people who might be interested in running errands. I have a few friends who would love to spend other people's money."

Gramps nodded and a smile tugged at the corners of his mouth.

"Just hush."

He lifted his hands. "I didn't say a word."

"What about your problem? Are you ready to introduce Brad to Tim and Carol? Maybe get your interfering children off your back about moving out of your house?"

"Ah. About that—"

But I didn't get to hear about Gramps' thoughts concerning the evil machinations of Aunt Carol and Uncle Tim, because Brad exited the house with a tall, brunette woman.

I examined them both for signs of distress, but they seemed fine. Mrs. Sherwood looked a little puffy eyed, but happy. And Brad looked relaxed. It must have gone well.

Gramps and I exited the car—one did not meet potential new friends while seated in one's car, if avoidable—and only when I was facing Mrs. Sherwood did it occur to me I was meeting Brad's mom. Brad, the guy I had feelings for, his mom. I was "meeting the parent" before we'd even had "the talk." What were we? Our relationship wasn't undefined, it was nonexistent.

As I quietly lost my bananas, Walter extended his hand and greeted Mrs. Sherwood, giving me a few extra seconds to get it together. She was excited to meet him, based on her smile and enthusiastic hand shaking.

"And this is Hillary," Brad said with a broad smile.

Mrs. Sherwood bypassed my offered hand and hugged me. It was the over-tight, I-might-not-ever-let-you-go kind of hug. The kind where you couldn't breathe and you kinda swayed a little from side to side.

When she finally let me go, she framed my face with her hands and said, "It is *so* nice to meet you."

She looked a little teary when she stepped away.

"Okay, Mom. I'll see you tonight?" Brad asked as he kissed her cheek.

She nodded but didn't speak, then hurried away. I was pretty sure that Mrs. Sherwood was going inside for a cry. The good kind, though.

"I guess you're coming with us?" I asked, though I didn't know where we were going or what we were doing. I hadn't gotten that far in my "what now?" musings.

"Of course, I'm coming with you. We have a social call to make." Brad opened the back door, but Walter waved him to the front before claiming that seat as his own. "Walter, I hope you don't mind that I gave my mom your number, since I don't have a cell phone. I didn't want to leave without giving her a way to get in touch, even if it's just for a few hours."

"No problem at all." And just then his phone pinged with a text. "She's just sent me a text so I'd have her information."

She had to be terrified he wasn't coming back.

"You're sure you should be leaving? That she's okay?" I asked.

"We're good." He climbed into the front seat.

"We're good?" I whisper shouted—but only in my head. What did that mean? Aloud, I said much more calmly, "You were only inside for a few minutes. What did you tell her? Why isn't she calling in the mental health reinforcements?"

"I asked her if she wanted the truth. She said yes. Oh, and she wants to meet Madeleine. She loves a good vintage dress." He shrugged. "That's what she told me, anyway."

Mrs. Sherwood was either in shock, or she was one seriously grounded lady.

I glanced at Brad's relaxed, handsome profile.

Having met her son, I'd say Mrs. Sherwood was a rock star. And likely incandescently happy to have her son back again.

Backing out of the drive, I hesitated, not knowing whether to turn right or left. "Wait, where are we going?"

Brad patted my knee. "To see Aunt Carol and Uncle Tim. Your choice who's first."

30

WALTER

They were so obviously in love.

Hillary was telling herself she was *on the path to* love, or some such foolishness, I'm sure. She'd shared her fairy godmother's plan: to allow Hillary to see the possibility of love. Also, a bunch of hooey.

Hillary and Brad were in love. They were a perfect match.

It didn't hurt that Brad had been nursing a crush on Hillary since the first time he'd seen her. Or that I'd shared all my Brad stories from the beginning, so Hillary had known the measure of Brad as a man long before she'd met him in person.

Truth be told, I was more of a matchmaker than that fairy godmother.

FG. Pfft. Who called themselves an FG? That was

even sillier sounding than fairy godmother. And it made her sound like she was ashamed of what she was.

I had mixed feelings about that Madeleine woman. The glasses were helpful. So was the summoning ritual, but she needed to up her game. I did the bulk of the work on this one.

"Gramps? What do you think? Aunt Carol first, or Uncle Tim?"

I leaned forward. This Italian mini-car really was more comfortable than I would have guessed. "You pick, peanut. I don't think it matters."

She muttered something about evil children or mad machinations, and I had to swallow a chuckle. She headed in the direction of Carol's house and handed her phone to Brad, telling him to text Aunt Carol and Uncle Tim that she was on the way and could they both converge on Carol's house for a family meeting.

Hillary didn't have children, so she didn't understand my relationship with mine. My children and I drove each other a little crazy. We had different priorities, different lifestyle choices, and different ways of expressing our love.

Tim and Carol worried about me and they loved me. To them, the solution was simple. Sell the big house with all the space I no longer needed. Put me somewhere with specialists who could watch over me and make sure my hallucinations didn't run rampant. Check the box that was me on their to-do list, and settle the anxiety my unsettled future caused them.

But growing older meant that the future was uncertain. Period. My health was excellent—now. My house still provided me the comfort of old memories without too much of a burden of maintenance—but that could change.

I had to admit, I was holding out hope that the big old house would be filled with the sounds of family—maybe even children—once again. That I wouldn't have to sell, because the house would find a second life with my loved ones.

But I'd broach that topic after the two young people in the front seat sorted out their path. It was clear as day to me. Paved with love and affection and shared values.

But they needed a little more time to see it.

I leaned forward again. "So what's the story? I don't think Carol and Tim will buy the fairy godmother angle."

Hillary laughed, which was exactly what I wanted.

31

HILLARY

"I choose you."

Brad grinned back at me from the passenger seat. "Okay."

I was floating on a bubble of good will, happiness, and pheromones. Aunt Carol and Uncle Tim had bought Walter's story about Brad being his roommate. I have no idea how. They shouldn't have, because Gramps had never been able to produce Brad before—hence their suspicions.

It was so completely improbable, so... *Oh, my.* So improbable as to be magical? I'd have to quiz Madeleine to see if she'd played a part in my relatives' acceptance. I didn't think she could interfere like that, but who knew?

That was the good will piece of my current euphoric state. Aunt Carol and Uncle Tim were appeased. Gramps psych eval was cancelled for the moment, and my annoying relatives had even promised to come by Gramps place for a monthly pot luck.

I turned my attention to the happiness and pheromone parts: the amazing man sitting next to me. Walter, Lord love him, had already headed inside, so Brad and I were all alone. Sitting in Walter's driveway in broad daylight—but all alone.

"You know I've got a bit of a commitment problem."

He didn't roll his eyes, and I had to give him credit for that. "You do seem to suffer from FOMO. Your four-business problem kind of hints at an inability to focus on one path."

"I do suffer from a terrible case of FOMO. But not with you. Promise."

The flirty look faded from his eyes. "I know. We haven't actually talked...about us."

"Isn't that my line? As the woman in the relationship, I feel like asking you where this is going is kind of my job."

He snorted. "Please. As if that's a man versus woman question. In case you weren't aware, that's a relationship question."

Just to be crystal clear, I asked, "And we're in a relationship?"

"I hope so." Then Brad leaned toward me, his

intent as clear as the affection and desire I saw on his face.

That little seed in my heart might be—just maybe—something more than a seed. It might be a proper plant, with roots and shoots and leaves. With all the growth spurts I'd been experiencing, I wouldn't be surprised if the dang thing grew into a tree before I could even catch my breath.

And I wouldn't be catching my breath now.

Nope, even if we were in Walter's driveway in broad daylight.

EPILOGUE
FIRST EPILOGUE: BRAD

Much as I adored my mother, I hadn't been able to envision living in the same house with her. It was *her* house. Her house, her rules. Which was exactly as it should be, and exactly how I didn't want to live my life as a twenty-nine-year-old man.

Good thing I already had a roommate I knew I could get along with.

Even better, he didn't mind living with me now that I was a lot louder, smellier, and dating his granddaughter.

On the plus side, I cooked half the meals and did a lot of the laundry. I even tidied up in between the cleaning lady's visits.

I wasn't a half-bad roomie, if I did say so myself.

And I was hoping I was about to become an even better one.

It had been six months since I moved in with Walter. I'd taken over Hillary's dog-walking and errand-running businesses, and after a few months bought her out. My mother had managed my savings for my missing three years, preferring to assume that without a body I wasn't actually dead. So I'd had some capital to invest.

I'd tripled the errand running services clientele, but I'd sold the dog-walking business. I wanted to focus my efforts. And I had plans for the profit I'd made on the sale.

About those plans...

"Walter?" I handed him a whiskey. "You have a minute?"

He gave me an inquisitive look but set aside his newspaper and took the drink, then indicated the living room chair opposite him. I didn't normally serve drinks for no reason, so he knew something was up.

"I've got a proposal for you."

He waited, looking unsurprised.

Here goes... "I want to renovate."

That took him by surprise, so before he could offer any objections, I explained. "You know I bought out Hillary's dog-walking business, built it up, then found a fantastic buyer for it."

He nodded, still looking taken aback. He hadn't even taken a sip of his whiskey.

"I got a really good price, and Hills wouldn't split the profit with me, because—"

"You did all the work building the client list, the app, and the scheduling system. I agree with her, if you care to know."

I shrugged. "Either way, I've got the cash now and wanted to spend it on something that Hills and I both would enjoy."

Walters eyebrows rose sky high. "And you think you'd both enjoy my old heap being renovated?"

"Well, yeah. Especially if Hills moved in." I blinked and tried to gauge his reaction. "And that's what I really wanted to ask you."

"If Hillary can move in to her grandfather's house?" His lips quirked up in amusement. Now he was yanking my chain. "You know she's welcome here."

"Yeah, I know that. No, I mean, I wanted to ask you..." My throat was suddenly dry as the desert. The Sahara was living in my mouth. I tried to swallow, and it didn't go very well at all. I had to just say it. Spit it out. "I want to marry Hillary, and I'd like your blessing."

A huge grin spread across his face. "Marry her, renovate the house, live here—live with an old geezer."

"Not exactly in that order." I wasn't about to renovate what I hoped would be Hills and my future home without my best friend, the love of my life, standing right next to me. She'd move in, we'd renovate, and then we'd plan a wedding...assuming she said yes. I was pretty sure she'd say yes.

"You modern kids."

I didn't roll my eyes, but it was hard.

Walter clinked his glass against the one I'd forgotten I was holding. "You have my blessing, and I couldn't be happier to see you make this house your home in every way."

Whew.

Now I just had to ask the girl.

I finished my whiskey in one large swallow.

EPILOGUE
SECOND EPILOGUE: MADELEINE

Being punished shouldn't be fun, I supposed, but did it have to be so hard?

Love wasn't my expertise. So, so not my expertise.

I was good at life, work, and family.

Love, not so much.

Though I was learning...I think. And I believed in True Love, which was more than I could say for many FG's specializing in love.

As for my supposed crimes against love, I stood by my innocence—even though I'd already been sentenced.

Was it really my fault that a couple or three's romances had gone awry on my watch? Their work lives had flourished, and their ties to family had strengthened. Those were very important aspects of human life.

I accepted responsibility for my failures and my mistakes. I just wasn't convinced those failed romances had ever been destined for success.

Hillary and Brad were a different story altogether. Hillary and Brad were True Love waiting to happen. They'd needed a little FG boost, but the components for a TL match had all been there.

Score one for True Love and the FG with the unconventional philosophy on love. (That was me, in case it was unclear.)

I had another match brewing that had turned out to be a little less conventional than originally planned. But it was a solid fit, and I planned to go forward with my FG intervention.

I'd have to keep it quiet. I didn't want the Council of FGs to stick their stodgy noses into my plans and ruin this wonderful couple's chance at True Love.

If the Council was going to make me specialize in love, then they could darn well live with the results.

Also, the results were awesome, because I was on the side of True Love.

Beth's love story, Skeptic in a Skirt, *is available now!* Keep reading for an excerpt from Skeptic in a Skirt.

EXCERPT: SKEPTIC IN A SKIRT

Best. Dream. Ever.

I was dressed in a gorgeous gown. And by gown, truly a *gown*. Never in my life had I worn a floor-length dress, let alone one made of a champagne-colored fabric so fine that the material alone probably cost more than my used Corolla, and that didn't even take into account the embroidered and beaded detail that was clearly hand-stitched.

And I would know—about the cost, the hand stitching, the fabric, everything—because my BFF Hillary was a professional shopper with excellent taste and a need to share all things fashion with her bestie.

What gown was complete without accessories? Or so the dream version of myself had decided, because I was decked out.

Gloves covered my forearms, past my elbow to the middle of my almost nonexistent bicep. (Someone needed to get to the gym more often.) The cool weight of a necklace rested against my neck. A flash of brilliance at my wrist had me wondering if I was sporting a matched set, and if I was—wow. If I wasn't dreaming, I'd be worried about getting mugged, even standing in a rose-scented garden with the gentle murmur of polite conversation and classical music trickling in from the distance.

Paranoid much? Nope. The stones on my wrist looked expensive. As in house-down-payment pricey. Big sapphires surrounded by diamonds, and there they were, hanging out on my wrist, looking fabulous.

I knew my jewelry, and this bracelet was gorgeous, vintage, and not crystal. I even had a rough estimate of its worth in my head. Like I said, house-down-payment-level wow, and that was just the bracelet.

My deep and abiding love of jewelry was a dark secret I kept squirreled away from Hillary. She'd have me "investing" in period pieces in two seconds flat. I was practical; she wasn't. I was a planner; she wasn't. I loved rice cakes; she loved Funyuns. I had a retirement account; she had four struggling businesses.

We were opposites, not in the ways that really

mattered when it came to being friends, but certainly when it came to men, money, and work.

But if Hills ever discovered my love of jewelry... I shuddered. She'd have my fiscally cautious side in detention, and I'd buy *all* the sparkly things. I wasn't usually susceptible to her spontaneous, Funyuns-eating influence, but throw a little bling in front of me and the combination of my bestie and my biggest weakness would be too much.

Speaking of sparklies, the piece of jewelry encircling my wrist begged for further inspection, admiration, and maybe a little stroking and petting.

I blamed my love of sparkly things and the exquisite beauty of the particular piece I was examining for my inattentiveness. Also, hello? Dream. Who paid attention in dreams?

That was why the voice caught me so off guard.

Two simple words: "Pardon me."

I turned. All right, I tried to turn, but floor-length gowns and I have never been on a first-name basis, and it didn't go well.

Strong arms and a spicy, woodsy scent enveloped me.

Did dreams smell good?

Whatever. I was dreaming, and my dream smelled amazing.

He smelled amazing.

"Excuse me."

That voice. My insides might have melted.

"Are you unwell?" the man attached to the very nice arms asked. *He* probably made it to the gym five days a week.

Wait...

Dreams didn't have lovely smells, nice arms, or British accents.

Grab your copy of Skeptic in a Skirt *to read Beth and Edward's story!*

BONUS CONTENT

Sign up for my newsletter to receive release announcements, bonus materials, and a sampling of my different series. Sign up on my website: www.CateLawley.com

ABOUT THE AUTHOR

When Cate's not tapping away at her keyboard or in deep contemplation of her next fanciful writing project, she's sweeping up hairy dust bunnies and watching British mysteries.

Cate is from Austin, Texas (where many of her stories take place) but has recently migrated north to Boise, Idaho, where soup season (her favorite time of year) lasts more than two weeks.

She's worked as an attorney, a dog trainer, and in various other positions, but writer is the hands-down winner. She's thankful readers keep reading, so she can keep writing!

Cate also writes under the pen name Kate Baray.

For more information:
www.CateLawley.com
www.facebook.com/katebaray
www.bookbub.com/authors/cate-lawley

Made in the USA
Monee, IL
26 June 2021